In Any Shape or Form

Short Stories

Pamela Mary Brown

Front Cover: Robert Caney—Underworld Scene with a Man
and Woman Enthroned and Death Standing Guard. Joseph F.
McCrindle Collection. National Gallery of
Art (images.nga.gov).

ISBN: 978-1548848682

'I resent violence or intolerance in any shape or form.
It never reaches anything or stops anything.'

—James Joyce

CONTENTS

Fly Away Peter—A Tragic Case

It was New Year's Eve when the pentatonic scale of *Auld Lang Syne* heralded a change in the weather to below freezing temperatures as people emerged onto the streets from the celebrations. The trees held shiny patches of ice on their branches. The roads glistened and snow began to fall at dawn. People moved about as if wearing slippers. At night, temperatures reached lows of minus seven and didn't rise above zero in daylight. The river froze. The snow was replenished nightly, falling in flakes like goose feathers. The coldest January on record since the big freeze of 1963 and coincidentally the year Paula was born.

FRIDAY

Paula walked toward the river that was shrouded in icy mist, and she clasped herself to keep warm. She hoped to find her pal and had seen neither hide nor hair of Peter for nights. She'd been beaten up and kicked, bore scars on her face and walked with a limp. Much of the assault had been

Peter's doing but others joined in because drinking sprees involve fist fights. Fights over money, fights over anything, or Paula having stumbled drunkenly into Peter and the bottle getting broken, the wine trickled into a pool and seeping through the cracks.

Paula returned to the old railway doubly beaten and tired. The marks on her face had the opposite effect on givers: they handed out less, repulsed by the sight of hardship, poverty and the facial evidence. Her usual sleeping spot in the warehouse had already been taken when she arrived at the nameless street. The sign had missing letters: 'est-en' Street. Paula hoped the intruder might move on, but when she slouched over the bedding he was sprawled asleep in a stinking pool of vomit. Paula kicked him and he waved his arms wildly connecting with her several times before eventually knocking her over. It had been a day when begging-hours were wasted on the two treks; to and from the city centre as she passed the heavily-armed shopping bag people queuing for those 70% discounts in high street outlets. Anyway, if Peter was sleeping it off, he would have been useless scaring away the intruder. All three would get drunk, and then the row where the intruder would receive a hiding from Peter.

'Peter, Peter,' Paula yelled which caused a sting of pain in her jaw.

Paula's physique was emaciated, shrunken and dishevelled. A coat draped over her body made her seem like a child playing dressing-up in adult clothes. She looked almost headless with the soiled woolly cap that had a wide turn-up of unravelling threads and holes in it as well. Her hair was a mesh about her shoulders and protruding through the holes of the cap. The biggest scar on her left cheek tingled. Her face had a blank look as if she peered from the recesses of a dark cave.

'Peter, Peter,' she called slumping near the intruder to snooze. 'Paula needs Peter.'

SATURDAY

On New Year's morning, the snowfall measured five inches on higher ground. Paula stopped to watch a mounted crane truck crunch through the hard-packed snow and blizzard, driven by a local business man transporting the derelict single room prefab. The truck lowered the prefab next to the old railway station building which was roofless. Paula arrived in time to witness the commotion that the ramshackle looking accommodation brought to the people who were staring at it curiously, knowing it would give them shelter. The prefab would be a change of scene from the old warehouse. Besides, one night with the intruder made Paula's decision free and easy.

As soon as the truck revved and backed out into the street, the new residents slowly established an atmosphere of comfort claiming their personal bed-downs indoors. Paula stood in the doorway, hidden in her pocket was the *Schooner Blended Sherry* that she had bought from the off-licence. To her surprise, Peter had found the prefab and was slumped against the wall, idly pushing his tongue between his teeth like a greasy salamander, lying sideways and shivering. Paula was shivering the more, but the day was looking up because of the new abode.

Paula tip-toed inside the prefab, hoping to stash the bottle, however Peter shouted at her demanding alcohol. She was cautious not to draw attention to herself as she wasn't a popular figure among the men. Paula stared impishly at the scruffy gathering who would drink from her bottle. The dry-drunks looked with disgust at her, sneering and wiping their noses on their sleeves. One man spat at her and Paula feared another attack.

'Clear off, you're not invited,' the drunk who spat glared at her.

'Get out!' Another shouted and threw an empty beer can. It hit Paula on the chest.

'This place is for members only,' someone said from the inner darkness and began to whinny with a laugh.

'It is my sherry,' Paula's voice was strained as she raised a hand beckoning to Peter with the bottle.

'Bring it here,' Peter rasped loudly as he banged his head against the wall threatening to unleash one of his fits.

'They'll rob me, Peter. They're dirty little robbers. Paula will give you the sherry.'

Peter stood up and was a hulking stooped figure but weak with a visible shake. He wiped his mouth and scratched his scraggy hair. His woodsman's beard was matted and nicotine stained. He stumbled above the men who were slouched against the grey walls of the prefab. No-one was threatened by him until his energy was aroused by drinking.

'Give it to me,' Peter shouted, and then pulled at the sleeping bag around his shoulders. His gloves were torn and his yellow fingers waxy and swollen with small blisters.

'Paula missed Peter. Why did Peter leave Paula?'

'She's your sherry, Peter,' the drunk who had spat at Paula said laughing out loud. 'Sherry baby!' He made an attempt at singing which turned into a bronchial cough and the red patches on his cheeks grew redder.

'Hell with you,' Peter dismissed the drunk with a wave of his hand, grabbed the bottle off Paula and opening it swigged with loud sucking noises.

'Do you want pills?' Paula pulled a jumbo packed of *M&M's* from the inside pocket of her cerise pink coat, tearing the lining so that it stuck out.

'Those aren't pills.' Peter held the bottle staring down at the others judicially. 'And who has a smoke, gentlemen?' A smoke to trade for a swig?'

But no one had cigarettes and the party atmosphere changed to one of siege. Peter returned to his position against the wall and Paula followed. She hunkered down and squeezed in beside him. When the others approached begging for a swig, Peter rose up like a phantom and repelled them. When Paula held the bottle, she took quick sips hiding beside Peter from the others. As soon as they finished the bottle, it was ceremonially broken against the wall and the issue was solved without further haggling. A broken bottle was empty. That was it. The bar was shut. The pub had no beer.

The warmth generated from their bodies heaped into the small space of the over-crowded prefab heated Paula up. She began to feel drowsy.

Paula opened her eyes wide feeling disoriented in a state of sleep inertia. She was groggy and her neck was stiff from the strain of sleeping cramped against the wall. Peter was no longer beside her and she grew fearful.

'It's chicken soup,' a woman standing in the prefab was offering Paula a Styrofoam cup. 'It'll help keep you warm.'

'Peter, Peter,' Paula called frantically knocking the cup of soup onto the Salvation Army volunteer who had a wooden tray with other cups.

Paula stumbled out of the prefab and off into the bitter cold. The sharp contrast in temperature made her dizzy. She fell over bumping into a man wearing a high visibility jacket, a hard hat and carrying a clipboard. The local council official quickly moved back and pointed at her.

'We need a court document to deal with these people,' the older official said. The younger of the council representatives wrote notes on a report form. He was embarrassed giving occasional looks at the prefab inhabitants.

'This dwelling breaks all health and safety regulations. The site is council property. We're liable. These people need to be removed. Simple as that,' the older official remained abrupt in tone.

'You can't just move them on,' one of the Salvation Army volunteers said—a woman with a round face, wearing a cap with a red band and a navy coat with a Red Shield logo. 'You'll be responsible if someone dies from hypothermia. Wait until the thaw comes. Then decide what to do with the people who live here.'

Paula ignored the Salvation Army volunteer and the offer of food and blankets. There was too much commotion for her. She pushed her way through the officials.

'Whatever bleeding heart dumped this prefab here is going to pay for it to be removed,' the older officer's voice was muted towards his younger colleague. 'A New Year's act of charity by some idiot and we're the bad guys.'

'The man who left it…his brother passed away on the streets last year. They say he is struggling with grief,' the younger officer added quietly as he watched Paula.

Paula staggered towards the river tripping, and stumbling until she caught hold of the steel railing. She looked at the embankment below, feeling as if she were moving on a boat. This disequilibrium added to her nausea and she lifted her face so that the icy wind numbed the feelings.

The gale had brought seabirds gliding inland to perch on top of lampposts. Others lined along the railing, their eyes in a fixed livid stare. Their presence and the stillness of the gulls made Paula calm for some moments and she gazed at them.

'I'm looking for Peter Marshall. One of the ladies over at the prefab told me you're also looking for Peter?'

Paula turned to find the younger council official had followed her. He was in his early thirties. A crest of the city on the right side of his jacket. Pens, and a torch in the top pocket. He held documentation in a cellophane file.

'My name is Brian. Do you know Peter Marshall?'

'Paula has sherry for Peter,' she said and turned her mouth downward as if she was about to cry.

'You're badly hurt. Do you want me to get a first aider?'

'Fly away Peter.'

'Excuse me.'

'Come back Peter,' Paula looked at Brian and her cheeks curved into a weak grin, but he had to stare sharply to see her face through the oval of the woolly hat.

SUNDAY

Paula heard the police sirens on the night of the second of January as she walked towards the old railway station located under the suspension bridge that looked like a giant white harp extending up into the grey clouds. She felt the insecurity of her tenure but such was her life. She blinked when she saw the blue flashing lights on the ambulance. Paula was returning to her usual sleeping place and hoped that Peter had chased the intruder away. They could resume the usual routine. Paula and Peter were long-time residents with fixed abode under a partially slated roof in one of the warehouses. A familiar couple to be sighted walking the cracked footpaths and overgrown railway tracks that sprouted sapling trees and weeds and attracted the clear–eyed seagulls swooping for throwaways by patrons from *KFC, Burger King* and the *McDonalds* Drive-In. Peter was her companion and as long as she could lure him with sherry he was her semi-permanent partner.

The police weren't an unusual presence in the derelict zone notable for clandestine high-crime meetings. Long cars drew up and the location provided anonymous space off the beaten track; to argue and make life and death decisions in drug distribution, car-prostitution and allied underground fast-financing activity.

When Paula noticed the police officer putting up the ticker-tape, she hurried to check out the hullabaloo. People's breaths condensed as they exhaled, forming little clouds in the air across their faces. A body lay on the ground with a coat covering the head and upper torso. The scene was like one of those from *Law & Order: Special Victims Unit* before the officials show up business like, as if nothing much has happened.

The intruder who had beaten Paula up on New Year's Eve had been restrained by Police. His hands were bound together in plastic handcuffs with two interlocking loops. He had caked-blood on the left side of his temple and on his hair. Two paramedics were cleaning off the blood but the man's head kept falling forwards as if in a state of sedation.

'Peter,' Paula called out and pushed her way through to where a police sergeant and a policewoman were interviewing Brian Marshall.

'He's my Peter,' Paula shouted, for surprisingly or not, she'd recognised her knight of the screw-cap bottle.

'Sorry, lady. You can't go over there. You know the victim? I'll need a statement from you.' the sergeant looked at Paula with little hope of being able to converse with her. 'Keep her here,' he said to the policewoman. 'Look at her face, she'll need medical attention.'

The sergeant stared candidly at Brian. 'You tell me that Peter Marshall is your father? The deceased is your father?'

'I've been looking for him since the weather turned cold. I was worried. I was gonna keep him with me, you know...well, if I could talk some sense into him. As soon as I got here, and saw him...I knew straight away he was...' Brian began to rustle his document folder. 'I'll have to, 'em, to make the arrangements,' Brian looked distraught and drained in shock. 'Does anyone know what happened?'

'I've told you that you can't go over there,' the policewoman was holding Paula back.

'I want to see Peter,' she demanded.

'I'll take her to the prefab,' the policewoman said and tried to guide Paula away.

'Peter sleeps for a long time,' Paula shouted at her.

'He's not going to wake up. He's dead,' the policewoman told her blankly. 'Come on. Look where you're walking, you'll slip and fall in the snow. If you get back into the prefab, I'll send someone to buy you a burger, chips and a mug of tea.'

'We live on the top floor at West,' Paula tried to remember. 'Yes, Westend Street.'

'There is no Westend Street near the old railway,' the policewoman said and turned to Brian. 'I'm sorry about your father. It's good to hear the area will be re-developed. The sooner the hoarding is up, and night watchmen in place, the easier our job will be.'

'My sympathy on the loss of your father, Mr Marshall,' the sergeant added.

MONDAY

On the third day of the New Year a Monday, Paula and Phil lurched towards a passer-by who had thrown money at them. Paula was out walking beside the traffic and commuters in their cars and buses. All the while as she walked, she looked towards the roofs and the tops of the buildings for the pigeons. She knew they were up there because of the cooing. These sounds changed her deathly look to a smile that was still broken. Her first shift of begging began around the bus station. People getting off the buses. People getting out of taxis. People carrying teas and coffees were not that easy for the first two or three coins. Mothers with children never gave anything, and old people walked slowly and pretended to look confused when asked.

And then the first hit of the day. A young man with a briefcase having taken a phone-call flicked a few silver coins at them as he rushed away. Phil's bulk wasn't enough to prevent Paula's stealth as she collected the most coins into her fist. As revenge, he kicked the loaf of bread that had the yellow *Reduced Price* stickers on the wrapper. A few slices fell out of the paper at their feet.

'You have enough for a bottle now,' Phil said tugging her arm.

Paula made an offer of Peter's sleeping bag, and Phil measured up to her former partner in every detail, except he was carrot haired. His clothes were dirty, torn and stinking. Paula and Phil walked towards the courthouse through the traffic and past the *Pound Shop*, *Boots*, two travel agents, and a four-star hotel. The statue of Lady Justice with her blindfold, scales and sword loomed from the balustrade on the roof.

Paula was exhausted after the weekend, but intrigued by the attention she was receiving from Phil who had begun to follow her in the early hours. She couldn't return to the prefab because she had been seen talking to the police and the old warehouse was cordoned off as a crime scene. Phil had suggested that she move into new living quarters. The debate was ongoing as Phil immediately saw the advantage of hooking up with this chief forager.

'We move tonight,' he said. 'Where's the bottle?' He demanded, grabbing her and beating the coat pockets which rattled the coins. 'Ah, you've struck it rich. Food and a bottle. We're in luck,' Phil was working on her.

Paula offered him some coins.

'It's freezing,' Phil wheezed and yawned patting his arms before pulling the sleeping bag tightly around his shoulders.

'Peter,' she said. 'Would you like a swig?'

'Oh,' he grabbed her. 'Where is it, then?' he asked loudly.

'Peter,' she shouted at him. 'The sherry is for Peter. You're Peter? Aren't you?'

'Look, Okay. I'm Peter. And you've agreed we're moving,' Phil said because he wanted to get some sleep.

'Okay. Okay,' Paula shouted. 'Peter, I have sherry,' she held the bottle by the neck diagonally sticking out from the lining of the torn pocket. 'See. Don't hurt Paula. Okay,' she pleaded.

Phil shuffled along beside her. Paula noticed a shop owner throwing a hulking mound of cardboard, folded up into flattened pieces, into the dumpster outside the *Today Shop*, and decided to beg.

'The cardboard's in there,' the young man said. 'Do you want me to gift wrap it for you?' He scoffed closing the lid.

Paula and Phil retrieved the cardboard and neither of them noticed the newspaper rack at the newsagents. Headlines still used the weather as front-page news: *Thaw Expected Late Next Week* fronted *The Daily Mail* backed up by a slender column:

'Old Railway, A Tragic Case'. Our correspondent has brought you, since the extreme drop in temperatures resulting in snow, sleet, hail, and treacherous road conditions nationwide, a spate of tragic deaths among the homeless. Most recently that of Peter Marshall, 56 identified by his son Brian at the old railway warehouses, a notorious Danger Zone, criminal and drug dealing location, also the hangout of many poor homeless citizens in our city, so hard-pressed at this time of year. Peter Marshall's death is under police investigation. His son Brian, tells of a father who succumbed to addiction, and mental health issues meant estrangement from loving family support. Brian Marshall helped the police to identify the victim. His father was found with a fatal head injury, and other torso injuries. A male suspect arrested at the scene was released without charge. Marshall's injuries are indicative of many factors; a fall with head impact on stone steps, or against a wall. The body was located in the broken doorway of a warehouse while the snowy-icy conditions mean a water-logged environment at the scene. The time of death is uncertain. Sergeant Craig Gordon said that 'this is a tragic event at any time of year and not least for his family.' The positive in this story is that the old railway is in the prospect of council re-development as offices, a shopping arcade, and underground off-street parking. Brian Marshall is a surveyor for the Council, and hopes to have among the public seating and leisure spaces a small plague in remembrance to 'Peter Marshall'.

Paula and Phil held the cardboard above their heads and walked into the recesses of the night towards the courthouse car park leaving birdlike tracks in the freshly fallen snow, and like everyone in the city, expectant of another morning.

The four-minute max theory

L arkhill Prison was five hours past lock-up at dusk. Clear landings and walkways showed in a concentrated glare of fluorescent lighting as the prison officers were making hatch checks. F-wing inmates had settled into what tuck-shop rations remained. TVs and radios hummed. Cell 27 had no sound system, no snacks and a twin-bunk discussion opened after a long silence with reading matter flung aside.

'Four minutes, max,' Frank spoke and his eyelids twitched excessively. He had developed rapid involuntary blinking during his trial, accompanied with unusual facial movements. The jury weren't going to be sympathetic, an open-and-shut case, but the spasmodic contractions of the ocular muscles made Frank look typically psychotic.

'One, two, three, *aannnd* the body relaxes,' Frank unclenched his fist slowly finger by finger. 'The fight's gone and hey presto, they're dead.' He swung his head over the edge of the top bunk to look down at Bobby. 'Men kill women all the time. Fact.' He clenched his fist once more.

Bobby nodded but his expression was blank. He desperately didn't want to engage with the conversation. He took his hands from behind his head and raised them to his chest, allowing them to fall crossed onto his body in the Lazarus reflex. And like Lazarus, he would require resurrection so that he could eventually leave this tomb.

'People say it's easy to snap.' Frank continued. 'But the thing is,' he rubbed his nose. 'I just wanted to do it. You know what I mean?' Frank lifted the corner of the beige quilt cover and blew his nose on the prison issue bedding. 'That's better. God, I hope I'm not coming down with the flu? This place is so bloody draughty. It's a germ factory. So, what were we talking about? Oh yeah, she's dead and I'm in here. A life for a life, as the old saying goes. But who knows how long anybody's gonna live? If I hadn't killed her, she could have got hit by a bus a week later. Anyhow, I got twenty-eight years. Serve a minimum of twenty-two.'

'That's a long sentence,' Bobby said and tried to imagine how he would feel if he was incarcerated for that many years.

'I knew what I was doing. I understood the consequences.' Frank added glibly. 'Lifers aren't usually doubled-up. But with the overcrowding, the number one Governor asked for a few volunteers. I thought a cell-mate would be no bad thing for a few months. I get an extra gym session as part of the deal.'

Bobby stared at the sheet metal base of the upper bunk after Frank swung out of sight. Frank's weight didn't impact on the solid frame. Frank was a small man with a rotund buddha belly, small hands, a bearded face and shaven head. Would he stand out in the crowd, Bobby wondered. No, he wouldn't. He'd probably inconspicuous, lost in the crowd.

The beds were bolted to the ground. The standard 7-square meters cell was a sterile environment. Frank had a point about the germs. The stainless-steel toilet and hand basin were only a few meters away from where Bobby lay on his bunk. He had been in prison two weeks and already gone through four changes of cell. Hoping for another move, he hadn't unpacked. His stuff was crammed into the small brown paper sack, his luggage gift-wrapped by the institution, and leaning in a crumpled bundle against the pale green-wall.

'The last guy I was doubled up with worked as a civil servant. He smashed his girl's jaw in. One clean punch. BAM. She was out cold. Her entire face was swollen. He thought she was dead, so he tipped hot chip-pan oil over her and tried to set her alight. Boy, did I laugh. And he assaulted the two female cops that came to arrest him.' Frank chuckled with a high pitch. 'Why would you send two birds to the scene of an assault?' Frank's snigger was lower this time. 'Beats me. Anyway, he swears he's rehabilitated. Said he'd been beating up on his girl for years, but she never followed through on any charges. So, he had no incentive to stop. Birds are like that...they can take a good kicking. Oh, and this civil servant guy cries in therapy, and it makes him feel better. He joined the happy clappers and he thinks she might even take him back when he gets out. That's birds for you. Me, I don't cry. And I ain't going to, either. My bird was asking for it. Stupid bitch. Know what I mean? What about you mate?'

'Oh, I couldn't hit a woman,' Bobby stammered and

scratched his track suit top.

'What are you in for?'

'I didn't pay a taxi fare.'

'What do you mean?' Frank gave an incredulous snort. 'How did that land you in this joint?'

'I fell asleep, and instead of taking me home, the taxi guy drove around for an hour. Then he tried to over-charge me. We got into an argument...someone called the cops, they took his side. A few blows to the head were exchanged. That's about the height of it.'

'I hope it was a good punch-up. Scumbags cops, the lot of them. Any female officers?'

'No. I wouldn't want that on my conscience. It got out of hand as it was. Well, more of a scuffle. I was drunk. They were at the end of their shift. I don't know to be honest, I was far too drunk, and I'd taken a winger.'

'Yeah, Man. There's nothing like an act of violence when you're high. When you're off your face, and the world is at your feet. I went to an FA cup final in Wembley a few years back. I stepped off a tube and nutted the first person standing on the other side of the train door. Boy did I feel good! Woo-hoo!'

Bobby cringed. How could he bide his time in this nut house? Keep your head down. Do your whack, that's what everyone said. The prisoners and the prison officers.

Bobby was assigned a number at reception, and the prison officers spoke to him using only his surname. The prison number created an alternative persona. He detached from life on the outside, it would wait for him. Or would it? He accepted his prison sentence. But prison was complicated. Many of the guys inside believed themselves to be normal. Was he normal? Prisoner D4526 incarcerated for common assault. Locked up with drug dealer, killers, psychos and paedophiles. Queuing for breakfast, shooting the breeze, and you've been talking to a child murderer about the weather. Tonight, he was in a cell with a man convicted of murdering his wife. What was normal in this place? There was a hierarchy of prisoners, that was for sure. The burglar was better than the drug dealer. The embezzler was better than the wife beater. And the common assaulter was better than who? He wished it hadn't happened, but it had and he would do his time, pay his debt to society.

'Look mate...they're cops. Male or female, it doesn't matter. They're all scum.' Frank said and pursed his lips. 'How long d'you get anyway?' Frank asked.

'Twelve months.'

'You'll be out in six. Keep your head down and your nose clean.' Frank said. 'Twelve months is wee buns.'

'Yeah, I'll do six inside, and the rest on licence,' Bobby said. He rubbed his face, then brushed his finger downward following the contours of his forehead and over his cheek bones, and on towards his chin. His mouth was dry.

'I bet the whole altercation didn't last more than four minutes.' Frank leaned over the bunk again, his face animated as he blinked.

'The assault,' Bobby said. 'Aye, it's all a bit of a blank.'

'You see, you are the perfect example of someone who demonstrates my four-minute max theory,' Frank continued. 'The worst of times and the best of times all last four minutes. Four little life altering minutes.' Frank swung back up out of sight. 'Two hundred and forty seconds. Tick-tock. Tick-tock.'

Bobby stared at the base of the upper bunk until the cell became a blur. He shut his eyes and tuned into the drone of TVs and radios, and the jangling keys, and the hatch checks and the buzzers and the footsteps on the corridors. He began to drift off to sleep, and life was happening somewhere further and further away.

'You can close a business deal.'

Bobby jumped in his sleep as if jerked by a rope.

'A doctor can diagnose you with a terminal disease.' Frank continued, and his tone was matter of fact. 'You can zone out to a great tune. Cook a microwave dinner. Roger Bannister ran the first four-minute mile.' Frank grunted and blew his nose. 'Oh yeah, and, apparently, it only takes four minutes to fall in love.'

Rubbish Night *or* Agnes contemplates the Feminist Movement, Reincarnation and Universal Harmony while putting out the household rubbish

gnes felt the invariable Wednesday night nausea and her stomach contracted. *Here it comes, here comes the night*...and she turned up the cuffs on her woollen cardigan, and she pushed her hands deep into the pockets, and she coughed, and she braced herself for the routine confrontation with her husband and teenage son.

In the sitting room, they were splayed lethargically on the sofa; their feet elevated on twin pouffes. Stained dinner plates, used cutlery and half-drunk glasses of milk were strewn on the floor.

'It's rubbish night,' her voice was an undertone to the blaring television.

'Give me that bloody thing!' Agnes's gruff husband grabbed the TV remote control from his son and tightened his lips as he turned up the volume.

'It's Wednesday night, someone needs to put the bin out.' She made the usual petition.

'I've just this minute sat down...he needs to move his fat arse...do something to earn his keep.' Her husband spoke and waved the remote control in the air.

'I've been following this TV series since the very first episode...I can't miss this one, Dad...' Her son snatched the remote control once again and looking at his father screwed his face up. His father reacted by returning a snide look. Their faces shared idiosyncratic snarls.

Agnes retreated from the sitting room, shutting the door quietly. She'd asked them for help and they'd refused, that was standard practice but when she didn't ask for help with a chore and commented about it later, they would berate her for not asking. Their bickering continued to be audible from the sitting room while the outcome was inevitable. Agnes had to put the rubbish bin out for collection.

The backyard light was faint and flickered inside a metal cage. The bulb would soon have to be replaced. The yard was small and the terrace house built on a slope in the late 17th century. The row had uniform fronts and Agnes' house was mid-terrace. The back of the houses lacked light due to the high retaining wall, and the small concrete backyard would have been put to better use as an artificial climbing wall for mountaineering enthusiasts.

Agnes cautiously mounted the steep steps to open the back-gate which sagged on its hinges. The gate creaked as she endeavoured to heave it upwards. It scraped along the concrete but Agnes had devised a method to manoeuvre it open just enough to accommodate the width of the bin. It had been a tiring day and this was the last of the chores before bedtime.

'Maybe I'll peel the potatoes for tomorrow's dinner,' Agnes muttered. 'I could put a pile of dirty clothes into the washing machine...hang them on the clothesline first thing in the morning.'

Twelve steps to the gate, Agnes thought as she returned to the backdoor of the house and gripped the handles of the wheelie bin, her back to the climb.

Step one, and she heaved and the weight of the bin increased her heart-rate and she thought about how when she first moved into the house an elderly neighbour helped her put the bin out each week. He had died of lung cancer a few years earlier. The last occasion she saw him he told her that his biggest regret was letting the surgeons cut him open.

Step two, and she thought about how her husband would drive over town to his mother's house on a Tuesday night to put her rubbish bin out for collection.

Step three, and she paused to make sure the load was tilted correctly and her balance accurately measured.

Step four, and she thought about never having planted a garden and how mature it would have been if she'd thrown in a few seeds or added a hanging basket.

Step five, and she thought about how life just seemed to be an uphill struggle.

Step six, and Agnes had to move her shoulders in counter-clockwise circles to ease the tension in her stressed muscles.

Step seven, and she wondered if her life would have been any different if she'd had a daughter, or a best friend or a sister.

Step eight, and Agnes thought about how frightened she was when leaving the house, but she had to get groceries at the supermarket. Her husband and teenage son never shopped for food, yet they stood by the open fridge door asking for milk, or eggs, or sausages.

Step nine and Agnes stopped, and she sighed and rubbed her hand across her brow, and she thought about what the *Feminist Movement* might think of her, standing on this very step with the heavy rubbish bin.

Step ten, and Agnes gripped the handle tighter and heaved the rubbish bin upwards with all the strength she could muster.

'Almost there, Agnes,' she whispered, 'almost there.'

Step eleven, and she thought about her great aunt's reply to her saying that if there was such a thing as reincarnation she would come back as a man.

'Why Agnes, are you afraid of work!'

Step twelve, and she thought about her triumph having made it to the top step and how another Wednesday would pass and she hadn't suffered a broken hip from a fall.

Agnes dragged the bin down the gloomy alleyway behind the row of houses, it was uneven and narrow but habit made the journey navigable. She placed the bin perfectly into a slot among the neighbours' bins awaiting collection. The bins were lined up numerically and in ascending order.

Returning to the house Agnes recalled how she thought about the same things every Wednesday night, week in, week out, year in, year out.

Agnes locked the sagging gate with the hinges creaking and walking down the steps she thought about how she would ask her husband and teenage son to bring in the empty bin the following morning. Neither of them would do it.

'Oh, to hell with it. The task will be much easier tomorrow,' Agnes said to herself as she closed the door and flipped the switch leaving the backyard in darkness. 'The bin's always lighter when the rubbish has been dumped out.'

Annual General Meeting

It was a frosty April afternoon when the siblings, two healthy bachelors and a wholesome spinster sat in front of the sagging door of the Stanley 9 cast iron range. The fire had been newly lit and a splatter of rebellious sparks projected through the grate and onto the concrete floor. Noreen lurched forward, her girth caused her to wobble unsteadily. She stretched out a hand and shut the fire box door. Cecil surveyed her cautiously. Noreen returned to her seated position and when she gave Cecil the nod, he tipped the tray of yesterday's ashes onto the floor. Alphonsus placed his elbows on the arm-rests of the súgán chair. He leaned forward clutching the poker with both hands. The annual McHugh family ritual of drawing out the farm was about to begin.

'Poor Mammy's broken heart,' Noreen said and shook her head from side to side repeatedly. 'Tut-tut, she just couldn't live without him.'

The death of both parents had occurred within a week of each other at the onset of winter. The dark nights that followed were passed with thoughts of grief as well as worry. The responsibility of maintaining the farm had been passed on to the McHugh children. It was the first time Noreen, Cecil and Alphonsus were charged with the management of the forty-four acres of prime agricultural land.

Noreen was especially shocked. She had always done her fair share of household chores. Could she extend this to outdoor work? She had hand-reared a dozen or so pet lambs but she had never milked a cow or planted as much as a handful of barley. She wasn't used to being out in the damp and rain and she caught cold easily. Noreen shivered and reprimanded herself; they would all have to buckle down and pull their weight. They were not helpless orphans but mature intelligent adults in their fifties. They had served their apprenticeship watching their Mammy and Daddy attend to the smallholding. Surely it would be water off a duck's back. Noreen's heart fluttered and her face flushed red. She would be taking the prescribed blood pressure medication for the foreseeable future. There was the livestock, and the planting, and the hedge repairs and God knows what else!

'This is how Daddy done it,' Alphonsus faked an air of officialdom. He skimmed the ashes over the floor until they looked like the outline of an undiscovered continent.

'So, what do we do?' Cecil's voice was squeaky and unused. He was the smallest of the bunch, the runt of the litter.

'We mark out the fields. Sure, didn't we watch Daddy do it year in and year out!' Alphonsus was confident. 'Cecil, do you remember the time you fell and the ashes went everywhere and Daddy was as mad as a rampaging bullock and we had to wait another night before he could draw out his plan.'

'It was you Alphonsus, you fell over! You were acting the goat!'

'Quiet! Both of you!' Noreen interrupted. 'We have to decide what we're going to do!'

'There'll be plenty of donkey work,' Alphonsus grunted. Then he paused, and as if transmogrifying into an esteemed calligrapher he wielded the poker in mid-air, brandishing it as a steel brush. Alphonsus rearranged the ashes to position the fields, the house and the barn in their correct geographical locations. This was done to scale. There was no need for mathematical calculations. Alphonsus had a keen eye. The ticking from three different clocks in the room competitively counted the seconds. Alphonsus was in no hurry.

'I bet you read my recent poem in the *Barn Door Monthly!*' Alphonsus said. He peered upwards, his statement directed at Noreen and his tone was goading.

'I did not.' Noreen's response was curt.

'Well, it was a timely poem, now that the planting season is upon us.' Alphonsus again looked upward but only momentarily. '*When the swallows return and the spring finds its voice, And the song thrush scatters his heavenly notes, we will plant with our faith, And tend with our joy, And the fields will bear the fruits of our prayer....*' Alphonsus recited his ballad with a haughty lilt. The words bounced off his tongue and the tapping of his right foot accompanied the recital.

'We can't plant your poems,' Noreen silenced him. 'And we're not here to make poems!' Just because she didn't entertain half the county with her poems didn't mean that she wasn't as good as him at making them.

Besides, Alphonsus loved annoying her and he had better handwriting and his poems were always neat and tidy on the page when he posted them off to the magazines.

'I think we should move the cows to the upper field.' Cecil was eager to bring the discussion back to the agenda.

'That's stupid,' Alphonsus said. 'Are you going to tramp the whole way up there to feed them? The fences at the top of the hill need mending. I say we leave the top field fallow. Plant it next spring.'

'But we need to move the cows.' Cecil objected. 'The grass is stunted in the lower field. The cows can't get their tongues around it. There's no hay left in the byre.'

'Put the sheep into the field the cows are in, and move the cows to the middle field.' Noreen said.

Cecil leaned back to think about this. He tilted the kitchen chair backwards until it was balancing on the two hind legs. He rubbed his hands together and wiped them over his stubbly face.

'What about planting?' Noreen had an authoritative air. 'Surely we need to put a few seeds into the ground.'

'I have to fix the tractor.' Cecil replied plonking his chair forward. 'That rope that holds the engine in place has rotted. We can't plough without the tractor!'

'*Old Moore's Almanac* predicts a bad summer,' Alphonsus added and shook his head. 'It'd be a waste of time to plant, everything will be washed away. We're better working with the animals this year and mend a few fences with the neighbours.'

Noreen and Cecil looked with suspicion at Alphonsus. He was cunning and up to something. He was a terrible one for talking to the neighbours, especially as he knew it was forbidden.

'Daddy doesn't allow us to mix with the other farmers!' Noreen said. 'He doesn't trust them.'

'Well, he's not here to stop us.'

Cecil began to whine like a scared puppy. 'I don't care,' he sobbed in a pubescent pitch, 'I'm not going against Daddy's wishes.'

'They laugh at us Alphonsus.' Noreen's said. 'I overheard them at the wake. They said the only thing we'll be able to grow is weeds. We need to stand on our own two feet...like Daddy and Mammy did.'

'But how are we going to run the farm if we don't work with other folk?' Alphonsus tried logic. 'I mean who's going to buy our cows and lambs?'

'Well, we could go to the mart like Daddy did. That's where he sold the livestock.' Cecil suggested.

'Go to the mart! THE MART!' Noreen's screeched and Cecil jumped. 'That's far too complicated, Cecil.' Noreen spoke in recollection and buried her face in her hands. 'I've only been to one mart and I lost Mammy in the crowd and Daddy said it was best if we didn't ever go back. He was mad as hell and Mammy didn't speak to him for a week, she was so scared of his bad temper. I'm going to *no* mart!' Noreen was resolute.

'I'll go.' Alphonsus was hopeful again. 'I'll ask young Heaney at the top of the hill to help. He said only a week ago that if we needed a hand with the digging, or anything, he had plenty of free time, now that he has left school. He's an up and coming man of the world!'

'I'll have to fix the tractor...that could take a few weeks.' Cecil poked his index finger inside his ear and carelessly flicked the wax that stuck to the tip. 'We need the moon in the first quarter and if I can't get the tractor...'

'Young Heaney can borrow his Daddy's tractor…and a trailer.' Alphonsus butted in. 'Them Heaneys have half a dozen or more machines. Cecil! You should see the modern equipment…it's like something off the telly!'

'I always fixed the tractor for Daddy. We never needed anybody's help.'

'Why don't we buy a new tractor?' Alphonsus blurted out the proposal. His burst of inspiration was far too hasty for Noreen's liking. Her expression became severe.

'We have money in the bank, and money under the mattress in Mammy's and Daddy's room, and we have money in the barn.'

'Speak a bit louder and tell half the county where we keep our money!' Noreen was enraged.

'All I'm saying is…' Alphonsus lowered his voice. 'We could easily buy a new tractor!' Alphonsus intended to continue with his petition but he fell quiet as Noreen hoisted her broad frame upwards. She put one hand on her hip and the other was suspended in mid-air, her stance as fixed as the statue of Lady Liberty.

'Buy a new tractor!' Noreen said in a hysterical screech. 'Have you completely lost your senses Alphonsus McHugh! You want to drive around half the country on a new tractor so you won't have to take your bike out on wet nights…you'll be running to wakes and dances and telling folks your poems. I know exactly what you're up to! Daddy didn't need a new tractor and neither do we! Cecil will fix the old one like he always does.'

Alphonsus opened his mouth to protest but Noreen spoke first.

'That's the final word on the subject!' Noreen had taken command of the meeting. She grabbed the poker from Alphonsus and aggressively poked at the ashes as if stabbing a wild animal's remains to make sure that it was dead.

'We'll let everything sit as it is for this year. Leave well enough alone…we'll get things in working order for next year. There's no reason why putting things off for another year will do any harm. We're still in grief.'

'But what about the cows in the lower field?' Cecil pleaded helplessly.

'Right, Cecil.' Noreen said. 'You better move the cows to the middle field, put the sheep in the lower one. They'll be nearer to the barn for lambing.'

Cecil nodded happily, he would spend the month moving them one at a time, swap them so to speak. That would keep himself busy for a whole month. The tractor would have to wait.

Alphonsus glared at Noreen and she responded with a look of scorn. He leaned forward awkwardly and opened the range door. It sagged heavily on its hinges near to breaking point. Alphonsus knew it wouldn't bear the weight much longer as he spat defeated into the fire. The spit sizzled on the burning wood.

Cecil took the poker from Noreen and scattered the ashes playfully. Noreen sighed, and placed her hands firmly into the front pocket of her apron. She stooped her head under the door jamb as she left the room to retrieve her blood pressure medication.

A soft whirring sound followed by a twitter-tweet caught the attention of Alphonsus and he titled his head sideways. He walked to the front window and mimicked the warble. Alphonsus strained his neck and looked upwards towards the roof. He saw two small birds with dark glossy backs, red throats, and long tail streamers. Alphonsus smiled wryly. The swallows had returned from their winter migration to roost in the eaves of the house.

The Doors of Imperception

In the waiting room, the receptionist didn't given me an upwards glance when I stated my name, appointment time and the name of my dental practitioner. I moved awkwardly to the seating area and sat on the edge of a grey plastic chair, beside the door. The chair tilted precariously and I wiggled rearward into the plastic moulding.

'It's hard to find a good dentist nowadays,' the man sitting across from me announced with a loud harsh voice.

I nodded distractedly, worrying about the on-street parking time limit. I had caught a glimpse of the traffic warden as I was going into the dental surgery.

'I'm jumping ship from this joint, as soon as I can,' the man bellowed as if addressing a public meeting. He folded his arms and leaned towards me. 'Did you know that only 10% of dentists are good at their job?' His eyes widened and he tapped the table with his index finger.

'Oh, that's low.' I muttered.

There were two women sitting beside us and their

eyes remained concentrated on glossy magazines. The frosted glass window and cool blue decor made it seem as if we were inside a fridge. I forced a polite cough, desperate for a diversion but neither woman altered their gaze.

'I know a dentist...he's alcoholic.' The man's voice was loud and incredulous.

'Oh, that's terrible.' I said and sucked air through my teeth making a slurping sound.

The man's face was drawn, and his coarse skin and wiry black hair made me think of my father.

'An alcoholic!' He emphasized loudly. 'If you hire a man to paint your wall...' He rubbed his hand over the wall behind him. 'You expect him to sand it down first. Then paint it. Don't you?' His voice was reproachful. 'But most men don't! They just paint the wall. It's the same with bloody dentists.'

I nodded as I attempted to decipher the nonsensical analogy. I was trapped in a verbal assault. I looked around in a last-ditch effort for an ally, but the other women continued to hold their reading material as protection.

'I got a call out late one night...' He continued, determined to dominate the air waves.

I decided to pick up a magazine from the low table. The gesture would demonstrate that I wanted his talking to stop. In a movement that nearly knocked me onto the floor, I managed to grab a battered copy of *Time*.

'A blocked sewer. This fancy doll opened the door. Aged about 45, but she looked 18 to 20.' He waved his hand from side to side in mid-air. 'Botox! She had spent thousands on Botox!' At the side of his badly shaven chin, spittle formed.

I stared at the cover photograph of *Time*. It showed a well-known political figure and I began to flick the pages.

'She looked really good. Like a woman in one of those magazines.' He pointed towards one of the women reading *Hello*. 'Then the husband came to the door. So, I said, "Get on a pair of wellingtons and gloves. You need to show me the septic tank." "Oh, no, no, he said. It's around the back of the house. You can't miss it."'

I focused on *Time* magazine reading a headline, '*Bully, showman, party crasher and demagogue.*'

'What a bloody mess!' the man's voice grew louder. He was determined to regain my attention.

I shut the magazine, felt defeated and rubbed my forehead.

'I got the thing cleared and when I went to the front door, she opened it again and took a step back...as if I might contaminate her. "Don't worry yourself, I said. It's done." Then I said something light hearted, but she didn't react. Not a twitch, except her eyes widened.' He made circles using his thumbs and index fingers and held them to his eyes. 'The husband arrived on the scene. "You're done", he said in his high and mighty tone. "I'll need another hour to clean up", I said.'

'Ok.' I nodded and re-opened *Time*. The magazine could be some sort of weapon, I imagined as I read another line, '*doing so allows him to give and take with the audience, to lose himself in the moment, orchestrating emotions like a maestro.*'

'He thought he was better than me, you understand?'
'Who?' I asked
'The husband. "Here" I said to him. "Do you know how much money I earn? £35 an hour! £75 for a call out!

That's £125...add another £35 cleaning up time."' He looked at me with a fixed grin, his gums and teeth were reminiscent of a horror movie poster.

'It's good money,' I mumbled and raised the magazine closer to my face and read another line, '*His sentences don't always parse, but they punch.*'

'I can't go out at the weekends,' I said to the Botox babe's husband. 'Too busy counting my money.' That put him in his place.' He shook his head and his face grew pale with resentment.

I half nodded. 'I'm going to read on, if you'll excuse me.' I waved the magazine in the air. 'This is a very interesting article.' My tone was one of apology.

'Later that night, when I was in my bed, the truth dawned on me.' The loud-mouth ignored my comments. 'That woman couldn't move her face because of the Botox. That's why her eyes bulged.' He once again made spectacles out of his fingers, and held them over his eyes. 'My joke did make her laugh. I'm a funny guy.' He lowered his voice. 'I found out later...she takes cocaine.'

I exhaled and tried to read another line about the politician. '*...wallows in a sense that the country is adrift in seas plied by cunning foreign adversaries. It is a roll of the dice in a garish casino.*'

The man leaned forward, uncrossed his legs and cupped his hands around his mouth staring intensely at me with a look of suspicion.

'Do you know what a carpet muncher is?'

The look of alarm on my face confirmed that I did.

'Oh, you do,' he chuckled with delight and slapped his thigh. 'I was doing a job last week for two prime carpet munchers.'

I closed the magazine in defeat. What was wrong with me? Why was I too timid facing the tyrant? Why couldn't I ask him to stop? I thought of my father again, and *Time* featured a strongman running for public office.

'I said to one of the dolls, "When I ask for your phone number give it to me in front of my mate." You see, my mate thinks that he's a bit of a psychologist. Always analysing people. He believed that he had the measure of the two carpet munchers.'

I began to perspire, the underarms of my blouse were damp, and my shoulders tense. The women opposite crossed their legs away from me and their shoulder hunched forward while their heads remained lowered. I shuffled uncomfortably. After my mother passed away my father transformed from a misogynistic bully into a frail old man. His bones were so brittle I could imagine him crumble into a pile of ash.

'We finished the job, and knocked on the front door,' he went on. 'The first doll had the cash to pay us. "Can I have your phone number?" I asked her in a flirtatious voice. I even gave her a sly wink. Then the mate says to her. "You look a bit defensive. Are you ok?" "What do you expect?" She snapped and she started hopping up and down, doing star jumps, and waving her arms crazy in the air. We left quickly. She was off her trolley if you ask me.'

A dental assistant in blue overalls called out a name. One of the women rose quickly and dropped her magazine onto the table. The noise startled me. I enviously watched her go into a treatment room.

'I'm a builder,' he confided in me. 'Maintenance work. Professional. Self-employed.'

'Oh,' I mumbled.

'Well...,' he paused. 'It's not easy, getting money out of people. 50% of the jobs you do. You don't get paid.'

'Oh, really.' I said and my voice was hoarse.

'One doll owed me £3,000. Accused me of not finishing the job! Next thing I know...I'm in the lock-up. Yip, she called the police. I end up in prison. They said I'd threatened her. If it ever happens again, I'll be put back inside.'

I nodded unable to speak. I was shocked that he had been locked up in prison.

'You meet all kinds in my business,' he said with a grin.

A treatment room door opened and a teenage girl came out. Her dark hair was tied up in a bun. She wore a grey and navy school uniform and she placed her hand gently against a cheek, massaging it.

'Dad, I've to come back in two weeks,' she said to the man sitting beside me. 'The dentist wants to do more work.'

'Okay love,' he said.

The young girl turned towards the reception desk. I hoped he would follow her but he remained sitting.

'That's my daughter,' he said. 'I have to look out for her. All kinds of weirdos about. My mate, the wannabe psychologist says, "if he had a daughter", he'd know where she was 24 hours a day. "Aren't you the smart man", I said to him. "24 hours a day!" Young ones tell you anything. You could drop them off at a nightclub, and they could wait inside the door and then go off somewhere with some thug.'

'It's tough for a woman.' I said watching the receptionist flicking through the pages of the desk diary.

'Tough!' he exclaimed. 'You don't know the half of it. You never know what lunatic is on the other side of a door.'

His daughter rejoined us, and he gave me a side-glance before he followed her outside. The surgery door banged shut.

I shivered and was relieved that he was gone. I picked up *Time*. I stared at the political figure on the front cover and then shoved the magazine into my handbag. I would give the magazine to my father in the nursing home.

King of Nothing Hill

Raymond Duffy pressed his foot on the brake pedal making a controlled stop at the cliff edge. It was a pitch-black night except for the car headlights shining their yellow saucers of light onto the guard-rail. The engine throbbed. He dimmed the high-beams and stared off into the murky land's end. He heard the squall from the waves crashing against the rocks below but was distracted by the gold wedding ring on his left hand. Raymond turned up the volume on the CD player and sighed.

Gonna close my eyes girl and watch you go. Running through this life darling like a field of snow...

He sang in time to the David Gray tune and tapped the steering wheel with the ring. The music filled the interior space and vibrated, making him feel as if he was inside a box speaker. He threw his head back against the headrest and closed his eyes. He needed the noise to drown out his thoughts.

Raymond collected his car from the dealership garage,

taking it without paying for the repairs done earlier that day. The sales manager had refused to give him the car, but Raymond had a spare key and returned to the lot when it closed for the night. There was a gap in the wall between the forecourt and *MacDonald's* where he drove through. If he'd made CCTV, he'd given it the middle finger. The sardonic thought made him grin.

'Damn him,' he muttered. 'I joined *The Beer Buff Club* online so I could send him a gift pack at Christmas. A guy has a tough month. Suddenly, no-one can do him a favour.' Raymond ground his teeth.

Raymond bought the hosepipe at *Homebase*. This finalised his decision. It was basic science. Re-direct the carbon monoxide from the exhaust. He imagined a passer-by finding the smoke-filled car at daylight. He hoped that whoever found him didn't look like his mother or father. He couldn't bare that, they would suffer enough. He was their only child, destined for greatness. The thought made him feel emptier, but it was too late to be concerned for anyone.

Tell the repo man and the stars above...you're the one I love...you're the one I love.

'You're pathetic, Raymond.' His wife shouted. His boss called him 'smug'. Work colleagues preferred 'smarmy'. The police report said 'letch'.

What the hell did he care? Raymond felt a surge of anger. He could face anybody. Looser, bully, idiot, thug. The list grew daily.

'Made it Ma! Top of the world,' Raymond imaged himself as James Cagney and looked into the rear-view mirror. The master delineator of criminal psychopaths, that would be a fitting obituary. But instead of seeing

Cagney, Raymond saw his matted hair as a black skull cap, the brown eyes bulging from lack of sleep, the melon shaped face, the fat lips always ready to trumpet his own praise, and his coarse moustache with trailing edges.

Raymond ran his hand across the dashboard.

'You'll never find an unhappy 3-Series man.' The sales manager had given a fake smirk.

Raymond still loved his car. He opened the glove compartment, took out a can of insect repellent and read the label. *Helps prevent and control the outbreak of insect-borne diseases. Malaria, Lyme disease, Dengue fever, Bubonic plague.* The seal was unbroken and he remembered buying it in the accessory shop. He had a vague notion of enhancing his travel experience. Thailand. The Philippines, or maybe Bangkok? He shoved the can back in and slammed the compartment shut.

Confucius says a diligent student needs no teacher.

Raymond snorted through his nostrils. He'd chosen teaching as a profession because the top teachers owned the top cars. Simple as that. Status elevation was a perk if you worked in an exclusive school. There was no point in growing old in some shitty school like the one he had attended. The pupils would have been better taught by social workers, behaviour therapists, and probation officers.

After finishing university, Raymond formulated a plan to get the teaching job he coveted by profiling the school principles of several elite schools. He investigated their extracurricular affairs and wanted to make himself known as a desirable candidate, even before an opening became available.

'Corpus Christi.'

'Amen.'

Derek Peters was a lay minister in St Paul's Cathedral, and a respected principal at an exclusive boys' school with its motto: *Sic itur ad astra. Thus one journeys to the stars.*

Tongue out, tongue in. Raymond received Holy Communion for two years, religiously attending 10am Sunday Mass where he looked as shiny as 30 pieces of silver going into the collection plate.

'Corpus Christi.'

'Amen.'

Raymond ensured he received the consecrated host from Derek Peters' Minister's hands. What was his crime? There was no crime to report, no issue of conscience to answer.

Tongue out. Tongue in and hey presto! A vacancy in the Science Department of the school where Mr Peters was Principal. These were jobs for life. Somebody must have retired or died.

'Goodbye shitty substitute teaching.'

Raymond felt both envy and admiration when he spotted the parking spaces reserved for the principal and vice-principal. Imagine a car parking space with your name on it.

'Wheet-whoot.' He whistled and strode boldly into his job interview.

Raymond offered a firm vertical handshake to Mr Peters who responded with a look of recognition. When Raymond sat opposite the panel in the lone interview chair he had never been so confident about anything in his life. He had rehearsed the spiel; the Catholic ethos, the school policies, the league tables, examination results and targets. The interview lasted thirty minutes.

'Corpus Christi.'

'Amen.'

Eighteen years later, and he was sacked from his cushy job. Mr Peters could no longer look directly at Raymond. He had spent a decade trying to find a contractual breech in order to fire him. There was a file of complaints from parents and staff. Debts had accumulated, there were rumours and an investigation.

Raymond no longer opened emails, letters, or answered his phone. His wife had changed the locks to their home.

'Open the fucking door Rebecca. I don't care if I wake every goddamn bitch-dog in the neighbourhood. I own this fucking house. I own you. I own the cat. I own every rag on your fake-tan back. You blood-sucking leech.'

Raymond gripped the steering wheel grinding his teeth. And he remembered it all. She called the police. *A police officer escorting you from your home—you cannot enter your own property*—there are no words to describe the anger. Everything you have worked for, gone. Okay, he had shoved Rebecca a few times. It wasn't as if she'd fallen down the stairs or broken a rib. She was a cold-hearted blood sucker who would have to flash a thigh to the loan sharks. It was a sure bet that they would be calling.

Tell the repo man and the stars above...you're the one I love...you're the one I love.

Raymond stared into the darkness and blinked as if something might appear. He was the King of Nothing Hill. Raymond revved the car. There was no going back. It took a lot of courage to...he still had courage...he would show them how courageous he was.

Don't see Elysium. Don't see no fiery hell. Just the lights up bright baby. In the bay hotel. Next wave coming in. Like an ocean roar. Won't you take my hand darling. On that old dance floor.

'Daddy?' A small voice spoke from the *Britax* car seat. The little girl stretched and wriggled. She sleepily scratched her legs through the pink fleecy pyjamas.

'Daddy? Are we going home now?'

'Yes Anna. We're going home.'

The Visit

'You can't go to that place!' Geoffrey shouted slamming the kitchen door. A cupboard snapped open and a plastic mop and bucket fell onto the tiles. Patricia nearly tripped up in pursuit to confront him.

'You can't prevent me,' she pulled on her camel coat and tied the belt viciously. Patricia caught a glimpse of her tinted blonde hair and tired face in the oval hall mirror beside Geoffrey's grey hair, the striped suit and pink shirt. The coat from *Bentalls* made her feel middle aged. His livid plump face reflected the weary GP. He gripped her upper arm. Fingers nipping into her skin. She was hurt emotionally and now physically. They were becoming patently criminal, she thought.

'I shan't be back until late tonight,' Geoffrey said in a rasping voice.

'Lucky you, tippling away at the golf club.' Patricia shouted.

Geoffrey banged the door into his den. He had

hidden the keys to both cars. There was no point searching. Patricia stepped outside and pulled the door shut. It was high noon and the sunlight glittered through the diamond pane windows on either side of the heavy mahogany door. The brick paver driveway was wet and the rain made her consider calling a taxi, but the neighbours would notice her loitering. Gossip was already insatiable about the scandal.

Patricia walked through Hawthorn Hill hoping to calm down on the walk into town. She couldn't recall the last time she had made the journey on foot. When her son Max was a baby, she often took him out for a stroll in his pram but that was many years ago. The breeze scooped up the fallen autumn leaves and scattered them again chaotically. It would be a long trek.

Patricia was peeved at facing the graffito slogans in the green tubular bus shelter. 'SCUM' 'SNITCHES GET STITCHES' 'BENEFIT TOUTS OUT'. The shelter had a gaseous stench of urine, piercing as ammonia. The metal rungs for the seat had been removed. Every Tom, Dick or Harry would know why she was at this particular stop. She managed a self-mocking laugh. At rotary dinners, Patricia often scoffed when the bus shelter was mentioned. It was known sardonically as 'the green mile stile'. The green mile, the short mile or the last mile a prisoner walks before execution.

Patricia was soon joined by women, children, and a few men. The women wore *Air Max* trainers and generic velour tracksuits. Many held plastic shopping bags which rattled in the wind. Cigarette smoke wafted from their faces as they sucked in and blew out plumes. They conversed noisily and shifted from one foot to the other.

Patricia hadn't smoked a cigarette since before her only pregnancy. Maximo, now twenty-three years old. She watched the children hopping on and off the painted kerbstones. They soon grew despondent and asked the adults about crisps, *Skittles* and fizzy drinks.

'First timer, eh?' A heavy woman said who smiled with protruding diastematic teeth. Patricia noticed the tattoo, a single rose entwined around a heart on her arm. Patricia shrugged awkwardly, feeling shocked at being called *a first timer*. She looked at the ground, sinking her hands deeper into her coat pockets as the bus came to a halt.

'You'll get used to it,' the woman gave Patricia's arm a gentle squeeze. Patricia sighed in exasperation as she opened her purse and stepped on board offering the bus driver a £20 note.

'Have you anything bigger?' The driver was sarcastic. He shook his head from side to side and grinned. His double chin wobbled as he chewed gum and tugged his bling VW earring.

'I'm so sorry,' Patricia said.

'How about a return ticket,' the driver's tone was kinder as he took the bank note, punched the coin holder and the ticket was dispensed. Patricia pulled it and blushed trying not to drop the coins.

Her legs wobbled as she grappled along the aisle to a mid-way seat. The seats were worn and dusty, making her nostrils itch. Patricia reached inside her coat to her trouser pocket and she felt for the diazepam. Geoffrey had prescribed the pills after the arrest. She found it impossible to be without them.

The bus passed the industrial zones where cars were

parked in lines. She read the signs high up on the buildings, repeating their names aimlessly in her mind. Apartment blocks faded into the distance. The bus drove on through bleak countryside. The road narrowed and the landscape opened up into flatlands with hedging. A sign with a green arrow indicated 'Perennial Lawns'. Patricia recognised the astro-turf company logo. Their vans were often parked at the golf club. Would Geoffrey believe she was brave enough to make the journey by bus? He'd easily picture her shopping. The shock had hit them. The gossip. More strain on their relationship. How could he write Max out of their lives?

Patricia saw clouds through the bus window and her anxious face with gaping eyes in the reflection.

'I can see the wall. I can see the wall. Look mammy. Look!' A young child was pointing excitedly out the window.

Patricia stared as the grey wall came into view. It seemed to be rising out of the terrain. Up closer it looked to be about 20 feet high, topped with razor wire. In her innocence, she thought the wire was like an overstretched slinky.

There was a reflective striped barrier outside the metal gates. The bus stopped in a gravel lay-by close to the barrier. The passengers got off the bus with plodding steps. Patricia was unable to stand. She began to inhale and exhale rapidly. Her heartbeat was audible and made her eardrums pulse. She got up and fell back onto her seat. The bus driver saw her in the mirror.

'Come on love. Do your visit. It does 'em good, you know.'

Reaching inside her trouser pocket, she removed a

diazepam. As she popped it into her mouth, the woman who had spoken to her at the bus shelter had climbed back on the bus.

'I'm Delilah,' she said offering Patricia her hand. 'Let's go.'

'My husband refused to come with me.' Patricia couldn't think of anything else to say.

'My old man's inside,' Delilah explained with a nod of her head towards the prison. 'Who are you visiting?'

'My son.'

'He'll be glad. You'll be fine. Thanks Fred,' Delilah winked and waved to the driver who rubbed his hands.

'Have a nice day, ladies.'

'Smile for the camera,' Delilah said as they followed the other visitors under the monitors and through a blue door in one side of the metal gates. Patricia stared at the high visibility yellow sign with '*Visitors*' printed in black and the regulations below. The text became a blur as she tried reading.

Inside with the others, each showed their visitor-pass and photo-identity. Patricia fumbled through her pockets and tugged out her pass. It had been folded many times. They moved forward selecting a locker.

'Number six is empty.' Delilah pointed. 'Put *all* your stuff inside. Lock it and take the key. Keep some change for coffee. There's a vending machine inside.'

Patricia was annoyed at the seasoned advice and felt repulsed by Delilah. The black dyed hair, dry and coarse. Her skin was darkened like leather from sun exposure. She imagined Delilah in Spain on a beach. 'Costa del Crime'. She had seen the documentaries.

The first three visitors walked single file into a

secured cubicle where several prison officers stood sombrely, one holding a black cocker spaniel on a leash. The far door opened and the three shuffled through to a bleak corridor.

'Next,' a prison officer said flapping his hand indicating that three more should come forward.

Delilah nodded with her head that Patricia should follow the heavily pregnant woman who had a toddler by the hand. The officer with keys secured at his waistband bent downwards and deftly locked the door behind them. The prison officer holding the dog moved as the dog led him towards Patricia. Delilah looked confused when the dog sat down next to Patricia.

'Your visit is cancelled. You won't get to see your son,' he said indifferently.

'What's happened?' Patricia asked.

'We need a female search team,' another officer spoke into his walkie-talkie.

'Ask for a boxed visit,' Delilah called back to Patricia as she went through the interior door that led to the corridor.

Patricia was ordered back to a holding cell by two female officers.

'Put your arms out,' the tall officer said with a downward stare.

'What have I done?' Patricia's voice was high pitched.

The officer carrying out the frisk quickly found the diazepam in her trousers' pocket.

'They're prescribed tablets. My name is on the label.'

'I need to see your visitor-pass?' The officer's stare was cold, her eyes narrowed and she unfolded the letter.

'I want to see my son,' Patricia's face was petrified.

'We decide if you can be permitted a visit. Your son's here for drug offences. You're smuggling pills into the visiting centre.'

'I'm not smuggling anything. Please.'

'We can call the drug unit,' the prison officer blurted out.

Patricia was silent as the officers conversed and went out. She stared at the magnolia painted brick walls, the green barred window frame and the metal chairs that were like cheap patio furniture. Patricia wondered if the room resembled Max's cell. He wouldn't let her visit when he was on remand. Max refused all her requests and Geoffrey refused to pay the bail or allow her to act as guarantor.

Keys rattled and the tall officer was in the doorway.

'You have ten minutes. Follow me.'

Max shuffled up to the glass partition. The thick glass was scratched and scored. He was wearing a grey tracksuit and blue T-shirt. Patricia sat on a stool that was secured to the floor. To her surprise, Max looked well. Before his arrest, he was using amphetamines and his weight had fallen dramatically. His face was no longer gaunt.

'You should have let me visit before,' she stammered directing her voice to a small grey speaker attached to the centre of the ledge.

'Don't Mum, don't go there. Forget it. How's Dad?' Max was curt.

'He's fine. He wanted to come but got an emergency call out.'

Max looked at her and believed the excuse.

'Max, how are you going to,' she went silent. 'Six years?'

'I can't actually plan the great escape, you know!'

'I don't mean...,' Patricia didn't know what to say.

'Look Mum, I'll probably do three years and three on licence. That's fifty percent remission. I've already served a year on remand. I work out in the gym. I've learned how to eat the slop they call food. I've got a job in the gardens. Don't cry...for God's sake...people will hear you.' Max leaned forward. 'Nobody in here cries.'

'I'm sorry, son. It's all a shock.'

A buzzer sounded and the officer called Patricia.

'It can't be. I've barely had any time...'

'Bring Dad next time' Max's voice was like a whisper. 'I need clothes. Will you put money in my prison account? For toothpaste. Tuck shop.'

'Visit's over.' The officer's voice was stern.

Patricia eyes were swollen from crying. The officers looked away as she took her coat and bag from the locker.

Outside the rain was still falling and the noise of the buzzer was ringing in her head. At the bus stop she felt disorientated and looked at the timetable.

'Medication?' Delilah asked with a knowing look. 'One of the officers told me you were in a bit of a state. Thankfully you got a closed visit.' She made a ghoulish face for a moment. 'They could have insisted on searching you further.'

'He wants money. Clothes.'

'Wha'd he do?' Delilah stared at the cracks in the tarmac as the rain began to lash onto the ground and seep into their shoes.

'Max was mixing substances in the halls of residence in Brackly College. Selling to students. He was under surveillance. He was caught with thousands in cash in a hold-all when they raided his room,' Patricia made a visor of her fingers over the eyes. 'Geoffrey, his father, refuses to visit him.'

'How long a sentence?' Delilah asked plaintively.

'Six years. He said he'll only serve three. Max is only twenty-three.' Patricia felt utterly abject. She stretched out her hand to feel the rain and went silent.

'We'll have a bit of a wait for the next bus.' Delilah looked at Patricia who didn't seem to hear. 'It's good to talk to someone who knows what it's like.'

Patricia still didn't respond. The far-off glow of the city in the dome of the sky was glistening steadily as Delilah set her hand gently on Patricia's shoulder. The day waned towards dusk and Patricia felt strangely calm for the first time in a year.

Anaphylactic Shock

I t snowed that weekend. The sky was Mediterranean blue with grey clouds whitened at the edges. The sun glared and it was almost impossible to look up at the sky. I was living in a cottage beside a river and the remoteness of the location makes it easier to quarantine. A tree lined avenue, an idyllic rural setting leading to a red door. It's a door that remains vivid to me and one that I'm afraid to reopen.

I never spoke about the violence. I left it behind when I left the relationship. I know it's not something you discard like an old coat or a worn pair of boots but I didn't want to bring it with me, not as a trauma or as an anecdote in intimate conversation. There is no way to assuage the details in the recounting. Language lets you down. I was shocked into silence and that's where I keep the violation.

Violence doesn't build up slowly. It's not a wound that begins to weep or gradually turns sceptic. It's just there and you manage it. You learn its traits. The irrational outbursts become predictable. Things fall over. You get shoved around. Insults are the poison that ensures you feel a level of responsibility for the duplicitous behaviour of the abuser. Physical, sexual and emotional abuse. Domestic violence is an unholy trinity that infects your mind, your body and your soul.

My son was born at eleven minutes past eleven. I liked the symmetry of the number. Eleven minutes past eleven. Now I close my eyes. Now I see his face. Now the fear overwhelms me. *His* explosive behaviour. My incessant worry. The sound of his footsteps as he approaches my consciousness.

'Open the door. I want to talk to you.'

If I keep quiet, he'll go away.

'I promise I'm not going to hurt you. Just open the door.'

Too late, the hurt already exists. It can't be given back.

He kicks the door. The wood splinters and cracks like a bone breaking. Screws are pried from their hinges. I try to scramble under the bed ridiculously but my stomach is huge. My pregnancy has almost reached full-term.

'When I tell you to open a door…you open the fucking door.'

My arm hurts. Fingers grip my skin and it reddens and I'm twisted around and dragged out from the bed.

Bang! My head hits against the wall. I am shoved tight against it. Fingers digging into my throat. The baby leaps and now I'm even more frightened. I desperately need to go to the toilet. I can't hold on.

'Let me go,' I scream.

His eyes narrow. His fist is in mid-air.

'Please, let me go, something's wrong.'

There is blood. There shouldn't be blood. What happens when your waters break? I don't know. I try to remember what the books on pregnancy say. They didn't mention blood. They discuss cramps and a bearing down feeling. What should I do about the blood?

The drive to the hospital takes 25 minutes. I sit on a towel and it quickly becomes damp. The traffic moves slowly. The road is wet and grey with slush. Cars follow the wheel-tracks made by other vehicles. Faces stare straight ahead. Their faces are featureless. How can they not read my mind? They should know.

The nurses don't know either. They ask no questions about violence.

'What time did you first notice the blood? How many weeks pregnant are you? Have you had any contractions? Can you lie on that couch? Are you the husband?'

I want him to go. I want him to leave. He whispers with the nurse. She folds her arms. They look over at me and nod. What do they agree on? More doctors, more opinions, more pain. The pain doesn't go away.

'You shouldn't have to suffer any more than you need to.' The nurse says and pushes a syringe into my thigh. Her hands are coarse.

I vomit. The nurse gives him a paper pulp kidney tray. He holds it under my mouth. I vomit some more. My nose runs. He wipes my nose. He is rough and it throbs and it feels like I've been punched. You can feel pain in more than one place simultaneously. I need to dissociate from the reality of all of this. There is a switch. Remember the switch. There. I am no longer who I am. I am no longer who I was. I am no longer a human being. I don't know what it is like to be treated in a humane manner. He grips my arms again. He pushes down. Are those tears? My eyes are blurred.

'Stop embarrassing me,' he snarls into my ear. 'You're hysterical. You're fucking off your head.' He pulls my hair from my face. The nurse stops what she is doing and looks at him.

'Any calmer?' The nurse doesn't speak to me.

He shakes his head and strokes my forehead.

'9 centimetres dilated. The doctor will be here soon.' The nurse snaps off the latex gloves, throws them into the bin and applies hand sanitation wash.

The doctor's white coat is too small in size for him. It makes him look like he has a dowager's hump. His arms are rigid. He has a long beard and thick Buddy Holly glasses. His dark hair is coarse and he scratches his head.

'Occipital posterior position.' He says to the nurse. They purse their lips tightly.

'Forceps?' The nurse demands impatiently.

'Give her another few minutes. If she used that screaming to push! She could do this by herself.' The doctor says.

'Is this going to be a 3rd or a 4th baby?' The nurse's look is stern. Her plastic apron has blood stains on it. 'It's almost eleven o'clock. Are you going to keep us here until midnight?' Her voice rasps at me.

Exhaustion. I've never felt such utter exhaustion. I want it to be over. I want to give up. I want to know what I should do. He stands behind me. His fingers rub my shoulders. I can't see his expression.

'One more push. A big one this time. Good girl...just

one more big push.'

My legs are in stirrups. They are raised high. The doctor is between them. He is sitting on a stool and leans forward.

'Head down and pant.' The doctor says with a sigh.

Head down and pant? I don't understand.

'Put your chin on your chest.' The nurse explains as she pushes my head forward.

The doctor holds a baby up. The baby is blue and covered in mucus.

'A boy,' the doctor says.

'Eleven minutes passed eleven,' the nurse glances at the white clock on the wall with the black digits and spidery hands.

They place the baby on my chest. He has a lump above his right eye.

'The swelling will go down, don't worry.' The nurse is certain. She brushes my arm.

I stroke the baby's cheek.

'What's the doctor doing?' I'm confused.

I feel strange.

Should I feel...' I try to speak. The room vibrates. The doctor has a needle.

'You need stitches,' he barks. 'Keep still.'

I shake and choke. My tongue is swollen. My eyes are itchy and feel like they are filled with grit. My skin tightens. He takes the baby.

'What's wrong with her,' he shouts. 'What's wrong?'

My lips are numb. It's impossible to breathe.

The doctor is beside me and lifts my wrist.

'Epinephrine.' The doctor shouts.

The nurse runs. A buzzer sounds.

I'm suffocating. Voices distort and my head spins. The buzzer is muffled. Someone pulls my arm. I've slipped through a crack. I'm no longer in the room. It's quieter here. I like the quiet. I can sleep now. I don't have to go back. I don't have to wake...voices...voices are trying to break through.

'Wake up, come on wake up.'

I won't go back to the pain. They can't make me go back. A buzzer or a cry? A tiny little cry. I know that cry. That cry is part of me. A baby. My baby. A boy. Eleven minutes past eleven.

'Okay baby, but only for you...'

And there it is. The familiar sting in my arms. I'm waking up.

***

The snow was falling when we left the hospital. He was driving and we didn't speak. The sky was overcast and the bare trees looked hardened. My son's newborn eyes blinked and were unable to adjust to the diffuse light. It was ludicrous to take a baby home in inclement weather. There seemed to be no road ahead, no horizon, no reference points especially on the back roads with no ruts for the wheels of the car. He parked close by the red door. I felt weak. His familiar angry bellowing.

'Don't drop the baby!'

He grabbed my suitcase from the car as I carried my son into the house. When he came in and locked the door I had a feeling of foreboding. I looked at the little baby in my arms. In a few weeks, I would feel much stronger. In a few weeks, there would be a change in the weather. In a few weeks or a few months or a few years...

My 'soul swooned slowly as' I 'heard the snow falling faintly through the universe and faintly falling, like the descent of their last end, upon all the living and the dead.'

Making a recurring visit in the same pyjama top

Morning sun glared on the glass fronted shops along the bustling high street making it seem like a house of mirrors. Commuters hopped off the buses that barely stopped, hissed and weaved back into the traffic. Workmen were grouped together, people emerged from the tube station, heels tapped the pavement, coats billowed and there seemed to be a coordinated pattern of movement. It was the atmosphere of somewhere to go, something to do, someone to meet.

Martha stepped onto the pavement and began to sneeze. She snapped open the clip of her handbag and pulled out a tissue. She rubbed her nose and shoved the tissue into her coat pocket ready for re-use.

'Sorry lady,' a heavy-set man said as he bumped into her. He was eating a bagel and crumbs flew from his mouth hitting Martha on the face. Martha brushed her face instinctively but having used her injured hand, the gesture caused a jolt of pain and she winced.

'It's ok,' she said and felt she may as well have been talking to herself. The man had continued walking and was out of ear shot. Martha sighed, averting her gaze from the younger commuters that made her feel tired and self-conscious. She'd barely time to dress and brush her hair since Ernest had slipped out of the house. She was a one-person posse and this would be Ernest's final day out and about.

***

'Count to ten. No. Count from ten backwards.' Ernest stopped walking and was trying to recall the sequence. He had sauntered along the crowded street and got as far as 'seven' but knew there were other numbers. He scratched his head bemused but couldn't feel any hair. What had happened? Who'd stolen his hair? He rushed abruptly and stared into a shop window almost snubbing his nose on the glass. His head was bald. His skin wrinkled. He started to pull at his cheeks. Somebody had stuck a mask over his face.

Ernest gazed up at the red Portland stone building. It seemed out of place against the steel and glass skyline. Where was he? Nothing looked familiar.

'Ten, nine, seven, eight.' The numbers were in his head, somewhere. Maybe he could punch them out. He began to slap the side of his head with one hand.

'Ten, seven, six.' That was better. He liked the number 'six' and his chubby toes wiggled delightfully. The gladiator sandals were on the wrong feet. He bent forward, and opened and closed the Velcro straps.

'Six. Six. Six?' Ernest called out and standing straight he stretched out his arms wide like the Angel of the North. He placed his palms upwards and turned 360°.

'There is nothing falling from the sky today.' He boomed loudly. His shouting caused a flock of pigeons to fly up across the front of the buildings. He flapped at the lapels of his trench coat wishing to fly after them.

'I can fly. Why can't I fly? Birds fly. Pigeons fly.'

The coat was too big for Ernest. He noticed his blue and white striped pyjama top underneath.

'Pigeons don't wear pyjamas.' He muttered and buttoned his coat.

Reaching deep into a pocket, he found a crumpled photograph and stared at it. It was an image of a young man standing outside a theatre with steps up to the glass doors and posters framed on either side. The young man's pose was relaxed, his hands rested on the belt of his trousers.

'I know you,' he said and tapped the image. 'Do you know me? 6th June 1960,' he shouted watching the faces in the crowd looking for anyone who might disagree with the date. No-one contested with him, so in a huff he tucked the photograph inside his pocket. He lurched off to the lower end of the street furiously pursuing a definite destination after a directionless morning.

***

Martha glimpsed her reflection in a boutique window. She certainly wasn't like any of the elegantly dressed mannequins with their aligned bosom and strings of faux pearls. Her body was square; she had short stick-arms and legs. A black polo neck highlighted her pale face and her white hair. She felt as if she was in a monochrome photograph.

'You could be a ghost,' she whispered as she touched the window pane feeling the lukewarm glass from intense sunshine. 'There you are! After all these years! Old haggard Martha!'

She began to smile, feeling sad, and she recalled the conversation with her doctor.

'Martha, you are bearing up wonderfully well,' the GP said. 'But he does need specialist care. Above all, you shouldn't feel bad about any of this, you know.'

'It is so far for me to travel,' Martha tried to interject.

'Look Martha, it's for your safety also...this isn't the first time you've been injured.'

'I would have to do an overnight stay, and I can't afford...'

'Let him settle in. You need to rest. The laceration on your hand isn't healing as quickly as we thought, now is it? I might have to prescribe an antibiotic if it hasn't improved by the time I see you on your next appointment.'

***

'Make-up? Yes. I shall need make-up. Make-up, then curtain up!' Ernest stopped abruptly, plonked himself down in the street and pedestrians looped around him sharply as if he were an open drain. He reached into the inside pocket of the grubby coat and retrieved a small make-up palette. The compact had a mirror on the upper part. Ernest deftly put his finger tip into the compressed powder and applied cobalt eye-shadow to each eyelid. He softly rubbed his finger over the upper eyelids so that the blue eye-shadow extended as far as his eyebrows. He applied circles of rouge to each cheek bone and used the same colour of red on his lips. He licked the tip of a stump of the eyeliner pencil, and made a small black dot at the left side of his face above the mouth. He snapped the compact closed and pushed it with the eyeliner into the inside pocket with great satisfaction. He stood up and happily hiked his trousers as far as they would go over his stomach. He tightened the belt firmly over his mid-rift and again noticed his pyjama top.

'How embarrassing.' Ernest sighed and tugged at the coat. He meticulously fastened each button. He felt satisfied that his pyjama top was tucked in. He goose-stepped off towards *The Strand.* Ernest was wildly swinging his arms up over his head.

Ernest stood to attention and saluted at what he expected to be the theatre building. He took the photograph out and looked at it.

'Where's the theatre?' Ernest looked suspiciously at the building and then examined the photograph again. 'The theatre is here.'

He stepped backwards into the middle of the road. Cars beeped and the noise made him cover his ears.

'Get off the road. Nutter!' A cyclist wearing a high visibility vest shouted.

Ernest stepped onto the pavement and waved the photograph at the traffic.

'It's not here. Did you see it? Someone's stolen it?' He was frantic.

Pedestrians, repelled by the sight of the unshaven face

with the horrifying make-up and tacky photo, avoided him. Those coming towards him and those past him, he obligingly turned to show the photograph to them all. A woman came out of the *Premier Fitness First*. He approached her.

'You stole it. You stole the theatre,' he accused her.

The woman was afraid, and clutched her gym bag tightly, she quickly brushed past him.

'I've no idea what you're talking about. Piss off.'

'She stole it.' Ernest pointed after the woman who rushed away along the street.

Ernest walked up the steps to the front of the fitness centre and made several attempts to move inside the revolving doors. It was as if he was dipping his toe tentatively into the ocean. Finally, on the fifth attempt he committed to entering and was between two glass panels in the cylindrical enclosure when the doors shunted and stopped rotating having hit his heels. He was stuck, hemmed in and banged loudly in great distress.

'Help, help.' He wailed.

A muscular man, mid-fifties, wearing a tight tracksuit with the *Premier Fitness First* logo approached, propelled forward by the swagger of his shoulders. He flipped a switch which set the doors moving again.

'You can't come in here. I've told you before.' He said bluntly and scratched his bald head and tugged the soul patch below his bottom lip. The small tuft of grey hair stood out against the otherwise clean-shaven face.

'That woman stole the theatre.' Ernest pointed to the street but his voice was a whisper as he squirmed.

'Look mate,' the fitness instructor pulled Ernest out of the revolving doors. 'You've been coming here too often. For the last time, the theatre's been gone for years!'

'But look,' Ernest held up the photograph. '6th June 1960. I'm here.'

'You're upsetting my clients.'

'But...' Ernest tried to speak.

'You can't harass my clientele. Come on. Outside with you. Right now!'

The fitness instructor nudged Ernest forward with his shoulder, forcing him into the revolving doors where they soon emerged back onto the street.

'My photograph!' Ernest bleated having dropped the photograph inside the building.

'Look here.' The fitness instructor gritted his teeth having lost his patience. 'What does that say?' He battered the metal sign. '*Pr-em-ier Fit-ne-ss Fi-r-st*!' He dragged Ernest from the entrance. 'I'm telling you mate, for the last bloody time. The theatre is gone. Shut down for years. Now bugger off.'

He shoved Ernest.

'My photograph.' Ernest shouted and ran back attempting to enter the revolving doors again but the fitness instructor barred the way. He stood firm like a bouncer outside a night club with his feet apart and his hands on his hips. Ernest bellowed and banged the glass with his fists, then gave up and sat down on the street and began to wail.

***

'Please, get the photograph. Will you please?' Martha asked calmly sitting down beside Ernest. She put her arm on his shoulder and pressed it gently. 'It will stop him

68

making so much noise.'

'Okay, lady.' The fitness instructor raised an eyebrow making his forehead wrinkle. 'I'll get the photograph, but he must stop coming around here. It's over. No more visits.'

The fitness instructor went inside. Ernest brushed Martha away and scrambled to his feet. Martha watched as he stood where he had posed for the photograph as a young man. Their first date when she took the photograph and they laughed so much that they dropped the camera. She thought it was broken. But the Kodak role of film developed perfectly.

'Here, take the damned thing.' The fitness instructor said as he pushed the crinkled photograph into Ernest's hand.

A police car sped past. The siren wailed. Ernest took the photograph, shoving it into his pocket as he stared after the police car.

'They'll be looking for you as a public nuisance.' The fitness instructor sneered at him. 'He has to stop, or I *will* call the cops.'

'Count to ten backwards,' Ernest said and took the photograph out again. He ignored Martha and the fitness instructor. 'This is me. I am here. I can see me.'

'It is you Ernest, I took it the day we...' Martha wanted to console him.

'6pm, 6th June...it's mine,' Ernest pushed Martha away and stared into the photograph as if it were a telescope. Martha stumbled outwards from the kerb towards the traffic and the fitness instructor quickly grabbed her with both hands.

'That bloke should be off the streets. I'm saying this

for your own good, lady.' The fitness instructor lowered his voice. 'Is he a relative of yours?'

'My husband,' she answered.

The fitness instructor nodded and he noticed Martha's injured hand and his face softened.

'He won't be around after today. I'm putting him into residential care.' Martha added.

'Well it's probably for the best,' the fitness instructor said and he sounded like her GP. 'Do you want me to call a taxi? Get him home safely?' The fitness instructor had his mobile phone out.

'No. I think we'll be getting along on our own steam.' Martha said and her voice choked. 'This is where we came on our first date and...that photograph, it's the only vague connection he has.'

'It's an awful disease,' the fitness instructor said.

'You know...he never liked the theatre.' Martha added and she wanted to cry. 'I suggested that we meet here.'

'I really think you should let me phone for you? Let's bring him inside. It can be my good deed for the day.'

They moved Ernest as if he might bolt out into the blue. They each held him by one arm and advanced towards the revolving doors. Inside the moving glass cylinder, they looked like three figures that might go around and around indefinitely.

Your Honour

Fumbling in the cargo pocket of his faded black trousers for the housekey Joe felt unhurried. The Housing Executive had changed their policy on self-closers. All front doors now required a mortise lock and door handles with a key. The inside had a thumb-turn fitted which was handy if you needed to make a sudden exit but impractical, according to Joe, because once outside you had to find the key to lock the door. Where was the logic? Health and safety gone mad, in Joe's opinion. Yet, his scowling neighbour who suffered from degenerative arthritis of the hands and was able to keep the self-closing door. It's the little things that could break you, Joe thought. He tugged the key from his pocket but the bottle opener keyring caught on the seam, turning the pocket inside out. Cigarette papers, filters and a chewing gum packet fell onto the doorstep.

'Ah,' Joe sighed as he slipped the key into the cylinder

and turned the mechanism until he heard it click. He didn't want an opportunist burglar breaking in to steal his prized collection of beer-mats. Among the many fine examples was a 1922 original from Watneys & Co., Stag Brewery, Pimlico, London. Beat that tegestologist, Joe smirked as he lifted the rubbish that had fallen from his pocket and shoved it through the letter box.

It was a damp day. Joe paused and tucked the hem of his trousers into his boots to safeguard it from the wet ground. He was proud of his Dr. Martens. 1914 Hi-Top 14-Eye boots. At one time, he wore the spare lace about his neck with a *No Nuclear* pendant hanging from it. Now the lace gathered dust on the kitchen windowsill. He had lost the pendant in a pub brawl. Man, was Joe still mad about that, the pendant had been procured by his uncle from an antiwar hippie during the Vietnam War.

Joe felt happier when he looked at his trousers puckered below his knees, it gave him the overall appearance of a rogue action hero. He squelched across the soggy grass. The local council had tried to engage the residents in the up-keep of the commonage. The initiative was supposed to bring about a marked decrease in neighbour complaints, anti-social behaviour, and crime. Involving residents from start to finish, according to feedback from similar initiatives, had increased awareness around social responsibility. Joe had helped plant a dozen cherry trees but local youths had set fire to them. He side-glanced at a circular patch of scorched ground and spat.

When Joe reached the bus shelter a fox terrier eyed him suspiciously.

'Are you waiting on a bus?' Joe asked and stretched out his hand to pat the dog on his brown oversized head.

The dog growled revealing his canine teeth and pink gums. Joe quickly withdrew his hand.

'We're all co-pilots on this planet. We might need each other someday.' Joe spoke to the dog until the 313 city centre bus arrived at the stop.

An elderly lady in a pink plastic raincoat disembarked, much to the delight of the terrier. Joe got onboard the bus and as it pulled off, he watched the dog jumping enthusiastically, following his owner.

***

'My Lord, might I beg your lordship...,' stuttered Mr McDermott QC tugging at the back of his gown, '...for an adjournment?'

'Tell me,' muttered the judge thumbing through papers on the bench.

'My client is only indisposed for as long as a ten-minute walk to get to court my Lord. As I've said, this is the third time, or I mean, it will be the third time that Mr Joseph Breslin will come before your Lordship.'

The case number Mr McDermott?' snapped Judge Norton.

'Breslin 70132. I feel we can have this settled with his Lordship in minutes.'

The judge gave Mr McDermott a cold look. Mr McDermott continued to tug the back of his cloak with both hands.

***

When Joe stepped off the bus onto the busy city centre pavement, he almost fell over Pigeon Woman.

'Don't touch my birds. Big ugly boots hurt my pigeons. Tut-tut-tut.'

'I'll fry all your pigeons and eat them,' Joe stretched his mouth open and screwing up his face, he stuck out his tongue.

Pigeon woman flapped a hand at Joe then shuffled off impervious, pushing her tartan shopping trolley and sieving the bird seed through her fingers. She was like a little hessian sack that was slowing leaking.

Joe tweaked his waxed handlebar moustache and stroked his dovetail beard. His sleeveless t-shirt exposed the Jake and Elwood Blues brother tattoo on his toned bicep.

***

'My Lord, if it please the court Mr Breslin hasn't arrived,' Mr McDermott hesitated and Judge Norton stared impatiently manoeuvring as if about to stand up. 'With your Honours' permission, when do we commence after lunch?'

Judge Norton ignored Mr McDermott and beckoned the court clerk with a flapping hand.

***

On the high street, Joe stopped outside a glass-fronted Barnardo's charity shop. He paused to read the WANTED CLOTHING, GOODS, & BRIC-A-BRAC sign. Smiling he recalled his previous visit when he bought a signed Van

Morrison *Hard Nose the Highway* 1973 LP. Joe imagined that the owner had died, and some uninformed audiophobe had cleared out his belongings without realising the value of the album. Their loss was his gain, ching-ching! Joe punched the air with his fist. Maybe he should try his luck today; maybe the charity shop had new stock, maybe another nugget that belonged to the dead fictitious Van Morrison fan.

***

'Your Honour...'
'Mr McDermott…'

***

Joe flicked through the LP's, rejecting each one while he grunted with disgust at the frumpy stars of the Irish Country and Western canon. Cheap Showband groups posed in 1970s wide collar shirts and denim flares. *Top of the Pops*; the female glamour model album covers, a series that ran from 1968 to 1985, 92 volumes in total. Joe was disappointed. Nothing, nought, zero, zilch, nada! He turned to exit the shop when a belt buckle caught his attention. Joe unhooked the belt from the rotating display stand. It had a silver ram's skull with the horns protruding upwards. Joe looked at the £9.99 price tag then he sneaked a look at the young student volunteer working at the checkout. Joe selected a plain belt from the display stand, removed the £2.50 price tag and casually changed it to the ram's skull belt.

***

Judge Norton entered the courtroom and sat down behind the bench. He had a refreshed look as he opened the buff folder. Mr McDermott rose like someone with abnormal convex curvature of the upper spine. McDermott faked a cough.

'My Lord, I'm afraid...' He hoisted himself upright trying to appear confident.

'Next case,' Judge Norton spoke to the court clerk.

***

Joe was tilting backwards and forwards looking at the ram's head belt buckle in the wing mirror of an Audi A5. The car was parked on a side street. The belt was genuine leather. It's the real deal Joe thought. He hiked up his trousers and rested his thumbs on the leather band. It accentuated his waistline.

'It's not the clothes that matters,' he said to himself. 'It's the hanger.' Joe smiled, making sure he caught his reflection in the car wing mirror.

***

Andrew McDermott looked through the wrought iron railings that cordoned off the courthouse from the pedestrian thoroughfare. Joe hadn't made an appearance. A warrant would be issued for his arrest. It was time wasted. Joe was an all-round waste of time. He wanted to close on Joe and the warrant now dropped him back in it. Where the hell was the bird-brain welfare hippy? He could have a thousand Joes but stuffy Norton ultimately could affect your career. He made sure embarrassment was maximised.

McDermott left the court precinct having noticed in the crowd a man fidgeting with a belt buckle. He quickened his pace, made several collision dodging manoeuvres past hurrying pedestrians, and reaching out he grabbed Joe's upper arm.

'Ah my favourite lawman, what's happening dude?' Joe grinned.

'There's a police car looking for you, follow me!'

'So, what's going on Mr McDermott? You said not to sweat it...I just had to be in court this morning,' Joe said following a fast-paced McDermott.

***

Joe and McDermott stood in the passageway inside the courtroom with some others behind a clerk as another case was in progress. They would have to wait with everyone else. McDermott shifted from one leg to the other and sighed. Joe winked at a woman wearing a grey suit with a pink and white stripped blouse and holding a laptop case.

Three members of the police looked at their notebooks.

'How did you see him first at eight o'clock when you say you saw him again at seven o'clock?' Judge Norton bellowed from the courtroom. 'Come, come, are you actually capable of reading the time!'

The court clerk turned to McDermott and nodded, then walked into the courtroom while McDermott and Joe followed.

'Your honour, my client's guilty on all counts,' McDermott said hastily, indicating that Joe should sit down.

'Mr McDermott, we are not hearing this case this afternoon. It was meant to be heard this morning.'

'I beg your Honour's time to say a word,' Joe spoke and raised a finger in the air as if he were a child in school.

'Speak.' The judge waved a hand flippantly and stared at Joe.

'Your Honour, I wasn't here this morning because I was minding my sick three-month old son. His mother's in rehab. She has a bit of a problem with the demon drink. The wee man was burning up. He's a colicky wee lad generally, but he had a temperature of over 102° and he cried all night.'

The judge indicated that he should sit down and be quiet.

'Mr McDermott, I'll dispense judgement under these circumstances as follows. Mr...,' he said looking at Joe.

'Mr Breslin, your Lordship,' Mr McDermott said.

'Stand up, Mr Breslin...we'll forgo the custodial sentence, remembering you're on oath from the first time you appeared before us. As a father, I'm impressed and hope that it will inform your intemperate behaviour for which I fine you on the three occasions collectively £250. You have a month to pay the fine or serve three months in prison if you fail to do so.'

***

Joe was waiting for McDermortt outside the courthouse. He was surprised at McDermott's lack of warmth.

'I don't think I can come up with £250 in six weeks,' Joe said. 'I've debts all over the shop.'

'There's a lot of things I don't know about you Joe. And a lot I don't want to know. You must pay the fine in the six weeks. If you can't meet the fine, to be perfectly honest...you'll have to do the three months.' McDermott was exacerbated. 'Your luck was in today. Judge Norton doesn't suffer fools lightly.'

'Don't worry about him,' Joe said. 'What does he know about life at the bottom. I had to put him straight'

'I never knew you had a son, never knew you were a father...we could have been better prepared in terms of the mitigating circumstances.'

'I've that road traffic accident claim filed and I thought your office would give me an advance.'

'In that case, and given the new information, we're going to have to write up your claim with the dependant...which, of course, changes things. I suggest you come to the office. Thursday at four. I keep that slot open to tie up loose ends before Friday and the weekend.'

**

Joe never showed up on Thursday at McDermott's office. He never paid the fine. He was released from prison after a serving a month due to good behaviour. It was only when he was up on a further charge of drunk and disorderly behaviour that Mr McDermott discovered Joe had no son, no daughter, no offspring whatsoever.

McDermott now had the added task of rewriting, yet again, the documentation on Mr Breslin's RTA personal injury claim. And at the next hearing, while they waited for his client to show up, McDermott had to inform Judge Norton of the reversal to the previous change in circumstances.

Joe had two lives: court life and street life. Norton and McDermott had the best of both lives.

Dead Starlings

'*BERNNADDEETTE!*' Dominic screamed like a multi-tentacled sea creature breaking through the surface of the ocean.

Bernadette's cheek was stuck to the faux leather upholstery and she pried it free, it left a sleep crease on her face. She was disorientated. It was early afternoon and an intensely wet Saturday. The rain bounced like water bombs off the bay window.

'It's time to wake up,' Dominic said as he walked calmly into the sitting room.

'How long has the weather been like *that*?'

'A couple of hours.' Dominic remained undaunted.

'I can't believe I've slept through it'. Bernadette flopped down again. 'I'd love a cup of tea.'

'That can be arranged.' Dominic pulled the pink and white stripped blanket over Bernadette and tucked it in around her body until her outline resembled a painted

Egyptian sarcophagus.

'You're so good to me.' Bernadette whispered.

'I love looking after you.'

Bernadette protruded her lower lip as a playful pout.

'You'd a late night.' Dominic said responding to her teasing. 'You're just a bit worse for wear.'

Dominic left the room which was spotless apart from Bernadette's discarded glad-rags that lay in a heap on the cream hearth rug.

'Eve kept asking me about you last night. She wanted to know where you were, what you were at.' Bernadette called out over the sound of the rain. 'I swear she's got her wandering eye on you!'

Dominic seemed in a good mood despite his raised voice to awaken her. Bernadette was worried as she recalled returning home in the wee small hours. She hoped that she hadn't caused too much of a commotion. She had a hazy memory of staggering out of a taxi, triumphantly getting her key in the door on the first attempt and then collapsing upon entering the hallway.

Dominic reappeared and, folding his arms, leaned sideways against the door frame. 'Eve is way too high maintenance. That's why she can't keep a man. I only have eyes for you.' Dominic laughed and moving forward bent over Bernadette, his shadow elongating like Nosferatu. Bernadette flinched and Dominic tossed her hair playfully before he left the room again.

'You have to come with me the next time.' Bernadette called out. 'It's not the same without you.' She lay back feeling relieved that there was no fallout from the night before.

Bernadette rarely left the house without Dominic, and

in particular to a pub or social outing, but the previous night he actually encouraged her to go. Bernadette strained to note his activities. If Dominic spoke she must understand what he said the first time. He could never be asked to repeat anything.

'Everything has a place. I like order,' Dominic told her early on in their relationship. At the time, Bernadette didn't realise that this extended to people. Three years later, and she was aware of her place but it was always a struggle to figure out what exactly made Dominic so angry. Everything and nothing.

Bernadette sat upright so that she could mentally account for Dominic's movements above the relentless clatter of the rain. Tea cups clinked and a spoon rattled. She heard a cupboard door snap close. Bernadette followed the trajectory of his footsteps as he returned; his lips fixed together in a satisfied grin.

'Your favourite cup...and just the way you like it!'

Bernadette took the teacup. Dominic sat down on the sofa, at her feet. He was precariously balanced on the edge.

'So, baby doll, forget who inquired about me? Who was fluttering round my pretty flower?'

'Nobody, well, nobody really...Jason was there.' Bernadette answered and took a quick sip of tea.

'Jason was there! And since when is Jason nobody?' Dominic kept his gaze on Bernadette. He took a mouthful from his teacup and swished it slowly between his teeth before swallowing.

'He's your friend.' Bernadette said.

Dominic snorted threw his nostrils at her.

'Was Fidelma with Jason?' His tone was aggressive.

'No. Jason said Fidelma wasn't feeling well either.'

'What do you mean, either?' Dominic screwed up his face.

'Well, I mean you weren't well.' Bernadette tried not to panic. She didn't want to over-talk. Her stomach knotted and her lips turned pale.

'But Jason was there.' Dominic added firmly as a matter of fact.

'Yes.' Bernadette replied.

'Did Jason buy you a drink?'

'Jason did *not* buy me a drink! I was in his company for a couple of minutes.' Bernadette felt dizzy. The noise of the rain was unbearable and she felt as if someone had pointed a hose pipe at the window. 'God damn the noise of that rain.'

'Forget about the bloody rain!' Dominic was irate. 'Tell me, what did Jason *think* about your new jeans?' Dominic added calmly.

'Stop it Dominic. I swear to God, this is ridiculous.'

'I'm not the ridiculous one, Bernadette. You wore those jeans going out.' Dominic stood up and picked up the jeans from the floor. 'I couldn't stop thinking about it after you left. It made no sense. You wanted to look good for someone other than me and I wondered who that could be.' Dominic tapped his left temple with his index finger.

'Nobody, I swear, nobody.' Bernadette pleaded.

Dominic held the jeans contemptuously in the air. 'You went *on and on and on* about how good you looked. *These are so stylish...look how they hug my figure...*surely somebody...even the bloody barman must have made a comment!' Dominic gripped a trouser leg in each fist and violently ripped the jeans in half. He flung them into the fireplace.

'I'm getting my smokes.' Bernadette said and tossed the blanket aside. She only managed to step one foot onto the floor before toppling awkwardly back onto the sofa from the force of the push that Dominic gave her.

'Stay there!' Dominic raised his arm in the air and then slowly lifted Bernadette's blouse from the floor. 'How many buttons did you leave open?'

'What?'

'What!' Dominic mocked her. 'The buttons on your blouse! How many were open?' Dominic tore off each button with his teeth, deliberately spitting each one into Bernadette's face before finally throwing the blouse into the fireplace.

'How long did you talk to Jason for?' Dominic was determined to get an answer. And the answer he required would have to corresponded with how he visualised the evening unfolding. He picked up his teacup and shoved it tight against Bernadette's breastbone.

'I need a cigarette.' Bernadette's voice was stifled as she tried to move.

'I'll give you a cigarette when you give me an answer.'

'Jason was in the bar when I arrived. I ordered a drink. He offered to buy it. I said no. We talked about you. Then I joined the women in the corner booth.'

Dominic swung his cup and hit Bernadette on the mouth. Her head flipped backwards.

'That's what you get for talking to strange men.'

'He's not a stranger.' Bernadette whispered and tried to sit upright. Her teeth throbbed. She could taste blood in her mouth.

Dominic swung the cup again, this time hitting it off

her temple.

Bernadette instinctively curled up her legs and held her hands protectively over her face.

'You were flirting with Jason.'

Dominic caught a clump of Bernadette's hair and yanked her onto her side. He placed one knee on the couch and one on Bernadette's hip. He hit her repeatedly with the cup while continuing to shout.

'Jason has my phone number...if he wants to know something...he can call me...you don't speak on my behalf!' The cup shattered against Bernadette's shoulder. Dominic flung the ceramic handle across the room. It bumped off the window drawing their attention to the darkening sky. There was a huge downpour and it seemed as if the house was being pelted by bricks.

'What the hell...!' Dominic shouted as the centre glass window pane cracked.

Bernadette tried to speak.

'Shut the fuck up, bitch!' Dominic gave her a final punch in the shoulder before walking over to the window to look outside. 'There are dead birds all over the front garden. What the hell!'

Bernadette winced as she wrapped the blanket around her body. She joined Dominic at the window.

'They're starlings,' she said.

'I'm going outside to figure out what happened.'

Dominic left the room and Bernadette continued to stare through the window as neighbours came out of their houses. Some looked to the sky, others looked at the birds.

Dominic joined them and chatted pleasantly while keeping his hands pushed deep inside his pockets. A few birds twitched and flapped. Most lay unmoving on the wet grass. The birds looked like lumps of coal.

Dominic left the gathering, removed his phone from his pocket and made a call. Bernadette turned away from the window. She lifted her handbag and retrieved her cigarettes. She lit up and shivered as she inhaled. Her mouth ached. She got a make-up compact from her handbag and stared at her reflection in the circular mirror. She had grey bags beneath her eyes. Her skin was taut and dehydrated. The jaw line was beginning to discolour. It was painful to touch. The previous bruises had only just faded.

'You get used to it!' Bernadette said softly to herself.

'Used to what?' Dominic asked coming into the sitting room and making her jump.

'Strange things falling out of the sky!' Bernadette replied.

'What are you on about!' Dominic said sarcastically. 'One of the neighbours has called the RSPB. It's the weirdest thing! We decided not to touch them. There are easily a hundred dead birds. Maybe more. There's blood coming out of their beaks. They could be diseased.'

'How could it happen?' Bernadette asked.

'Who knows! Bloody birds. Bloody pests.'

'But dead birds don't just fall out of the sky!' Bernadette added.

'Well, the media are on their way! It's going to be crazy.'

Bernadette knelt on the rug in front of the fire. She picked up the tin of Swan lighter fluid and squirted it over the torn clothes in the grate. She threw a match on top of them and watched as the clothes disintegrated beneath blue and yellow flames.

'Those fumes could be toxic,' Dominic said. 'You haven't a clue about anything, do you!'

Bernadette ignored him.

'Oh.' Dominic added casually about to leave the room. 'I've good news, Fidelma called my mobile while I was outside. She sends her apologises for last night. Like myself, she was feeling under the weather. Anyway, Jason gave her a full report. There's absolutely nothing to be upset about. And they've invited us to dinner. Next Saturday evening.'

Bernadette continued to stare into the flames.

Mansfield House

B rigadier George Wilson raised a confident hand to speak.

'Of course, it reminds me of meeting Mr Churchill.' His face altered and became downcast as he grabbed his chin in confused recollection. 'It was either in Plymouth or Southampton?'

'Yes, Brigadier Wilson. We know you met Mr Churchill. It's time for bingo. You need to take your seat. Come on Georgie Porgie.' Frank gripped George's upper arm and led him quick time across the floor of the common room. He shoved George onto a seat among the other elderly residents.

The room had been a ballroom before Mansfield House was converted into a care home. It still had the marble fireplace and high windows facing onto the three-tiered garden. The wallpaper showed a tracery of vines with sparrows and starlings. The furniture was practical as many of the faux leather chairs had restrainers to prevent people falling. The sliding sash windows had net-curtains on the lower halves. The room was lit from dusk to dawn and used for insomniacs. The pictures suspended from the picture rail were a series of landscapes and cityscapes with captions high up on the wall. The bookcase with paperbacks, CDs and DVDs was topped with a TV screen always on like the ceiling lights.

Nurse Rodgers was issuing the bingo books and pens. With her usual smile to the residents she made a flirtatious glance at Frank who had sat at a table with the *Super Select Electronic Bingo* machine. She snapped each bingo book securely onto a blue clipboard and got everyone's attention with rebukes and reprimands.

'There you go Josephine. You had a bit of good luck last week. Pauline, stop the giggling and take your book. Margaret, remember to clean your mouth after dinner. Use the hanky tucked up your sleeve. Don't spit on it, Margaret. Wilfred! Keep your hands to yourself. Oh dear, Brigadier George.' Nurse Rodgers placed the final clipboard on his lap; not impressed with the military man or his former rank.

***

A door opened. George staggered into the garden. His steps somnambulatory as he mounted the wheelchair ramp leading to a fountain with wicker chairs. The ground was wet. His slippers were soon soaking. The lawn was the length of a bowling green. The laurel hedging swelled in growth that required pruning. Rhododendrons gone wild blocked out the light. Insect life and wasps in summer and late autumn threatened everyone outdoors. George arrived at the fountain feeling frail and fatigued. A flowering weed lured him to sniff it. Margaret liked flowers. Who was Margaret? If he touched this flower maybe he could go and look for Margaret.

'George! BRIGADIER!' A male voice bellowed.

George pulled the flower out of the ground by its soggy roots.

'George!' The male voice again.

Suddenly, a pain in his arm.

'I took a hit. Retreat to the ridge, men. Hold back. Defend the house. Move out of the line of fire.' George cried out and stumbled forward.

'He thinks he's in the war,' Frank laughed. 'Brigadier. Enemy snipers over there. Retreat in single file!' Frank said mockingly as George tried to resist his grip.

'No, Georgie.' Nurse Rodgers shouted. 'Frank needs to get you inside.'

Frank pulled George harder and he fell over onto the wet grass.

'I'm not going to make it,' his face was frightened as he begged for their help. They did, but roughly.

***

'My father's face is bruised!' George Junior was distraught at Nurse Rodgers who held a bundle of medical reports.

'Your father fell out of bed. Again.' She replied. 'Isn't that right, Brigadier?

The bed rails were raised and George with his eyes open stared at the ceiling.

'My father's in bed in the middle of the afternoon!'

'He's been asleep on and off all day, and refused to attend our gala bingo,' Nurse Rodgers's voice was harsh.

'You can't lock him up like this.'

'And he fell during a walk outdoors after lunch,' she said stolidly as Frank entered the room.

'Surely there is supervision?' George Junior turned on Frank who leaned by the door with his arms folded.

'It's for his own safety, he's quite a handful,' Frank grunted.

'Mr Wilson. I understand your distress but Mansfield House has the highest standards. Your father is particularly high risk. His dementia is not only a danger to himself but other residents.' Nurse Rodgers added.

'Pigs,' muttered the Brigadier.

'What's that Dad?'

'Mr Churchill shook my hand.'

'That's right Dad,' George Junior took his father's hand.

'Did I tell you what he said?' Brigadier George's eyes were wide.

'I know what Churchill said, Dad. You told me. About the pigs, and the cats and dogs. Churchill told you that "Dogs look up to us. Cats look down on us. Pigs treat us as equals."'

'No,' Brigadier George cried out. 'Pigs treat you like pigs.'

Statement of Complaint from Eleanor Kelly concerning Mr Richard Carmichael of the Children's Court Council.

The gross infringement on the Human Rights of I, Eleanor Kelly during the recent Court Contact Agreement concerning my daughter, Anna O'Brien (age 8) and her father Sean O'Brien, follows in the Timeline:

8 May

First appointment with the Children's Court Officer (CCO), Richard Carmichael (hereafter 'Carmichael') already arranged by phone between Sean O'Brien (hereafter 'O'Brien') for Anna to attend his office. Anna was taken into a room on her own with Carmichael to talk about her feelings regarding access with her father, O'Brien. Anna was stressed after the meeting and found the experience upsetting.

11 May

Carmichael was present at the Court Hearing in B— when Contact Agreement was negotiated. (I have never denied nor intended to deny Anna access to her father). In Court on the day, O'Brien actually negotiated LESS access than he had been granted when we first officially separated. There was no reference to his previous unreliability concerning access when he did not arrive to collect Anna, or sent text messages cancelling access.

Inside the Court on this occasion, Carmichael referred to me as 'formidable and uncooperative'. I felt his comments were personal, untrue and unprofessional. O'Brien claimed having Parental Responsibility granted him a-hands-on role in Anna's education. This was backed by Carmichael.

Background Note to My Statement of Complaint: O'Brien refused to let me liaise with him regarding school matters. He was asked to leave the school grounds on a number of occasions by the school principal. The Board of Management at Anna's school requested that O'Brien liaise with me in order to receive school reports, etc. They didn't want their pupils continually exposed to his aggressive behaviour. Anna had been tested for Asperger's Syndrome (though not diagnosed with the condition) and was receiving Special Needs help at school. She is a particularly quiet child but as soon as O'Brien moved out of the family home, Anna's schoolwork began to improve.

7-8 June

Carmichael telephoned me to discuss access and the issue

of joint Parental Responsibility regarding the school situation. During the phone conversation, I told him that I had decided to leave the area. (I had always planned to move to live near my sister Amy in N— for support). The move involved a 2-hour commute.

Carmichael's reaction was one of annoyance at my decision. He stated that my motives were 'suspicious' and my behaviour 'depressed him', not just as a father himself, but in his official role as CCO. Furthermore, he complained that I let my feelings interfere with the situation and that 'my reactions were unnecessarily emotional to all court situations and procedures'. He further stated that if I showed 'less emotion' the situation could be resolved and agreements adhered to. I was extremely upset over his comments.

Carmichael was aware of the Barring and Protection Orders that I had taken out against O'Brien. Carmichael had access to my hospital file which listed the injuries and the assaults on me by O'Brien.

A further court hearing had been set for the 29 June at Carmichael's request. He wanted to amend the Access Agreement to ensure that contact continued.

29 June

The morning of the Court Hearing, Anna gave me a letter written on a school copybook page. In her letter, she said that she did not want to be interviewed by Carmichael anymore. This letter was refused entry into my portfolio by the Court.

The Case was adjourned until the 23 August. O'Brien and I were instructed to speak with Carmichael. My Statement of Evidence regarding my relocation had to be submitted to the court by the 18 July. The Statement must include the following: my new address which was to be with my sister Amy, her husband and children. Anna's new school, medical services for her and details of Amy's husband's work and earnings, what sort of accommodation Anna would have in my sister's house, as to whether she would have her own bedroom. Carmichael was instructed by the Court to interview myself and Anna on 2 August.

2 August

Anna ran upstairs when Carmichael arrived at my house. Carmichael interviewed me in the kitchen. He asked personal and intimate questions about my relationship with O'Brien. I was aware that Anna was sitting on the stairs as she often does. I was anxious in case Anna would hear any of the replies to Carmichael's questions. At Carmichael's insistence, I had to coax Anna downstairs to speak with him.

Carmichael demanded an interview with my sister and her husband who I would be living with in N— . I told him that I would have to see about this because my sister and her husband would either have to bring their children or find someone to mind them. To help me get through the court proceedings, Amy and her husband very kindly agreed to travel to B— for the forced meeting to take place at Carmichael's convenience in his office for 2pm on Monday 6 August.

6 August

Carmichael arrived 30 minutes late to the meeting. Amy and her husband attended the meeting and answered his questions truthfully about their life, earnings and their children. They described the dimensions of the bedroom where Anna would sleep at night, the food they usually ate, the school, and whether a house with two extra people would prove 'inharmonious' which was one of the words which Carmichael used. He also stated that it was strange that Amy's husband would accept a sister-in-law and her child staying with them.

23 August

The Court agreed that they could not prevent me from moving and leave was granted pending a review and subject to an interview by Carmichael with Anna on 26 October. I demanded of the Court that I be allowed to accompany my daughter to the interview with Carmichael which was granted by the presiding Judge. He also agreed that the meeting should take place at a 'neutral venue'.

26 October

O'Brien phoned me at 10am saying that Carmichael had arranged to meet Anna at 2pm on 29 October. The location was designated as O'Brien's mother's house where O'Brien lives, in St Dermot's Close, B—. I listened without complaint but had to agree and said 'yes' in order to end the phone call.

I decided to phone Carmichael's office to explain that Anna begged me to be with her at the meeting. However, I was informed that Carmichael was on leave until 29 October.

29 October

At 9.30am I phoned Carmichael's office and after 20 minutes on hold I finally got speaking to Carmichael. He initially rejected my plea that I accompany Anna to the meeting arranged for O'Brien's house. I told Carmichael that my Legal Aid solicitor assured me I could bring Anna to the meeting. Carmichael stated that he did not have written confirmation of this statement nor could he recall the judge granting permission. The meeting was to take place in a neutral venue. I asked why he considered O'Brien's mother's house to be a neutral venue.

Carmichael informed me aggressively that O'Brien could exercise his Parental Responsibility and object to me taking Anna anywhere. He said that O'Brien and he had decided that my being at the meeting with Anna would result in conflict. He recommended that I allow O'Brien collect Anna and that I keep away from the meeting.

During the phone call, Carmichael stated his reservations about my move to N— and stated that my motive was only to take Anna far away from her father. Carmichael stated that he had 'after all' only met my sister once. I was unsure as to what he was insinuating about Amy. Carmichael did not take into consideration that O'Brien had a partner who had never been interviewed or called upon, and whom Anna is in company with during access visits with her Dad; these visits include overnight stays.

Carmichael was annoyed because I hadn't given O'Brien the address of Anna's new school. Anna had missed the first two weeks of the school term due to my having to wait for her application to go before the Board of Governors of the school. He did not allow me to explain that it has taken weeks and various pressures as it would be for anyone to relocate to find a suitable school, especially under the commands and behest of the court with O'Brien harassing, and scrutinizing my every move and perturbing me whenever he made contact over access.

I told Carmichael that I would not go against my daughter's wishes and the meeting would only take place if she was comfortable with the surroundings and those present. He eventually backed down. Carmichael said that he would confirm matters with O'Brien. He demanded that I attend at his office at 1.30pm. Carmichael demanded to interview Anna on his own, and then to interview me with Anna, and then me on my own again: three meetings in all. This was made as an order to be carried out.

Anna was interviewed for 10 minutes on this occasion and when Carmichael returned her to me he said that Anna was *well adjusted* and there were *no further issues*. I was unsure as to whether he still wanted to interview me and when he said nothing else and kept silent, I took it that I could leave. As I got up to go, Carmichael relayed a message from O'Brien which was a pick-up time for Anna that evening. Here again were O'Brien and Carmichael arranging together for O'Brien's access time with Anna. Such a scene made me highly uncomfortable at the level of contact between O'Brien and Carmichael over Anna.

2 November

Court hearing scheduled for 2 November which would finalise access arrangements due to the relocation. Unfortunately, due to illness and childcare restraints I was unable to attend. In any event the new agreement was not granted at that court hearing as my Legal Aid solicitor informed me. After which I received this communication which reveals the sort of pressure I felt:

Submissions were made to the court that Anna did not attend school for one month and until recently the father had no idea where the child was attending school. The Court Children's Officer, Mr Richard Carmichael confirmed that you were unhappy with his continued involvement. He expressed concern that at the present you are only facilitating contact as proceedings are before the court and he fears that with the ending of the court proceedings that contact with the father will come to an end.

The case has been adjourned for further review on 30th November. Your attendance at court on this date is required and you should arrange to be in attendance at court at 10am on 30th November.

Note: Carmichael's statement was both worrying, coming to me as it was through my solicitor with the stated concern "that at the present you are only facilitating contact as proceedings are before the court […] and with the ending of the proceedings that contact with the father will come to an end."

This statement was totally untrue of my actions. It is unjust and violates my human rights as a responsible mother, and as a law-abiding citizen. I have always been concerned to maintain Anna's contact with her father, and having moved with my daughter, enable access and contact at my own expense in terms of petrol costs and also in terms of travel time. O'Brien provides me with minimum maintenance, the basic amount which is a legal requirement. In terms of clothes and other financial necessities regarding school, O'Brien refuses to meet me half way.

Anna says that she is happier in N— more than she ever was in B— and loves her new school, friends and the teacher which is a considerable leap in both her recent good spirits and her ability to adapt to big changes in her life.

Anna feels betrayed by Carmichael and has stated that Carmichael 'lied' the day of her interview when he said that there *were no further interviews*. Anna wanted to know 'what did she do wrong?' On the morning of my final hearing, Anna said to me as I was leaving to attend the hearing that she wanted to come to the court with me as there was nobody to 'speak' for her in court, ever, and that she was 'not important'.

The exhausting, long drawn out intrusion into our lives over the year has caused me and my daughter high levels of distress. I never had, nor ever intend to prevent access between Anna and her father. I emphasised this fact continually and I went above and beyond the access agreement made in court.

During the entire process, nobody had taken into account the fact that Anna's needs and wishes have always been at the forefront of my actions. If I prevented access with O'Brien this would be detrimental to my relationship with my daughter, as I know Anna wanted to spend time with her father and I wanted to ensure that this was maintained at all costs.

30 November

The proceedings came to an end. Carmichael still emphasized that I would stop access. He never gave an explanation as to why he held this bias and prejudice towards me since access continued according to the court Access Agreement and with extra arrangements by me for Anna to be with her father over Christmas.

During the final court proceedings, Carmichael's assessment of Anna stated that my daughter was a 'Crowd Pleaser' and this phrase was read into the final court statement by the presiding judge. This term is highly inappropriate and dangerously intimate for a Court Children's Officer to make about any child especially within court access proceedings. Carmichael's psychological assessment of my daughter as a 'Crowd Pleaser' fully amplifies my terror of Carmichael as a Court Children's Officer holding a responsible position in an irresponsible manner through his actions, conduct and behaviour towards Anna and myself.

Carmichael's role as CCO was supposed to determine and speak for the wishes of Anna. His belief that Anna is a 'Crowd Pleaser' further serves to justify Carmichael's behaviour. It negates anything my daughter has ever said as part of the court process. It in effect took away the voice of a bright and articulate child who said: "The day my Dad took you to court was the day my childhood ended."

13 December

When O'Brien was arrested for questioning he confessed to the murder of my sister, Amy. The Police informed me that O'Brien murdered Amy believing she was me. He had stayed in a B&B near N— after a recent access period with Anna and began stalking the house at night. The location of the murder weapon—a gun—he has also made known to the police. My brother-in-law and his children are inconsolable. The murder is all over the *Evening Herald*, other newspapers and on TV. My life is devastated and unreal.

A number of months have passed since the tragic loss of my sister. We are unable to pick up the pieces. I want this statement to be fully addressed by the *Court Complaints Department* and request that Richard Carmichael be removed from his post with immediate effect. He was complicit in the murder of my sister, actively encouraging O'Brien to aggressively pursue and continue to bully and stalk me throughout the legal process.

Learning to Fly

Sarah grabbed the handbag off the roof of her yellow 1975 Vauxhall Viva car and scanned the busy street with small shops on either side. Her habit of absentmindedly leaving the handbag there was a town joke. She, of course, would laugh at herself in public, but privately Sarah believed that the incidents didn't merit the level of small town hilarity that it repeatedly attracted.

'Did you see her driving around with the handbag on the roof?'

'It's the second time this week. 'Tis well she doesn't drive faster than 20 miles an hour!'

'She'd be in a better line of business selling handbags to herself, than tights and knickers to the aul biddies.'

Today Sarah didn't want to be the focus of ridicule. A 'delicate matter' had been brought to her attention and was causing her grave concern. She had to talk to Alicia before the gossip started. Sarah closed the hosiery shop in the early afternoon. The bell over the front door made a soft jingle as she pulled the door shut. Her small business brought in enough income to give her a decent wage and keep Alicia at school.

'Give us this day our daily bread...' Sarah prayed before starting the ignition. Perhaps Alicia was right. She should upgrade the car. Buy one that was a less conspicuous colour and move with the times into the 1980s. But Sarah couldn't part with the car; her late husband had bought it a few weeks before he passed away. He shouldn't have been driving at all, given the amount of alcohol he consumed daily. Thanks be to God that he left the car at home on the day he was called to meet his Lord and maker.

Sarah drove to the nearby school bus-stop. She parked on the roadside and watched Alicia nonchalantly hop off the school bus. Alicia was engrossed in conversation with a group of boys. The girls crossed to the other side of the street and Alicia looked relaxed among the boys. It made Sarah feel happier. If the stories were true, then surely, she would be on the other side of the street along with the girls?

'Oh, sure you can't be up to the young ones nowadays.' Mary McIlroy said to Sarah earlier that morning.

Recalling Mary's comments, Sarah beeped the horn. The school children looked toward the car and when Alicia noticed her mother she bolted across the road.

'Are you alright Mammy?'

'Get in, love. I'll explain all en route.'

Alicia looked anxious; she open the door, threw the bulky schoolbag into the back and sat in the passenger seat.

'What's wrong?' Alicia asked.

'Nothing's wrong love.' Sarah's response was abrupt and then her tone softened. 'I want to take you on a driving lesson...you've been nagging at me for weeks. Mary McIlroy was in the shop this morning, she told me about an ideal location.'

'Mary McIlroy?' Alicia's voice was shaky.

'The one and only!' Sarah's answer was high-pitched.

'Where'd she say we should go then? Alicia asked.

'The runway, out at the new airport. Apparently, after four o'clock the workmen finish up for the day. The place is unoccupied until six, before night security come on duty!'

'I can't believe it. Mary McIlroy is good for more than the occasional pair of ladder resistant tights.'

'Yes...Mary was a mine of information.' Sarah's tone reflected how outraged she had been at Mary McIlroy's morning broadcast. Mary had stared at Sarah triumphantly while putting her change into her purse and snapping the clasp shut.

The journey to the airport was completed in silence. Sarah sat forward on the edge of the driver's seat holding her hands at the ten-to-two driving position. Alicia stared out the window at the pastoral landscape of east Mayo.

The airport had been five years in construction and was finally nearing completion. Sarah drove in through the wide entrance and past the elongated terminal building, the control tower, and entered the runway. She stopped the car just over the threshold. Two and a half miles of flat concrete strip stretched out before them.

'We can change positions now.' Sarah unclicked her

seat belt, opened the driver door and walked around the back of the vehicle. Alicia walked around the front. They eyed each other, as if in a Mexican standoff over the hood of the car. Alicia got into the driver's seat and Sarah climbed into the passenger side.

'Clutch, brake, accelerator.' Sarah began the instructional speech.

'Mammy...' Alicia interrupted. I've been through this a hundred times. How many times have I played taxi driver?'

'It's not a game this time.' Sarah said reproachfully. 'You're going to be driving for real.'

Alicia confidently put the key into the ignition and started the car engine. She revved and accelerating slowly. The car began to move forward. The manoeuvre was smooth. The car steadily gathered speed and when it reached twenty miles an hour Sarah felt her heart flutter.

'Don't go any faster now Alicia...this is your first lesson...don't be overzealous love.'

'For God's sake Mammy...there's not another car in sight...this is a straight road...what harm can a bit of speed do?'

Alicia accelerated to thirty miles an hour with Sarah gripping the door-handle.

'Stop Alicia...stop...you're going too fast.'

Alicia increased the speed to forty miles an hour.

'Stop, stop!'

Alicia didn't stop and accelerated some more. At fifty-five miles an hour Sarah placed her hand to her heart.

'Stop, Alicia, in the name of God STOP!'

The speed continued to increase.

'Mary McIlroy said you were caught kissing a girl in

school!' Sarah screeched.

In a state of panic, Alicia grabbed hold of the gear stick and thrust the car into first gear. The engine roared and as she pulled the handbrake the rear of the car skidded, sending the vehicle into a tailspin. It rotated several times before coming to an abrupt halt. There was smoke from the rear tires and the smell of burning rubber.

'Mary McIlroy doesn't know anything about anything!' Alicia protested.

'Then, tell me it's not true, Alicia. Mary McIlroy said that Father Rooney caught you and another girl in the science lab at break-time...you were kissing each other...on the mouth!'

'Father Rooney's a pervert. Mammy he's always spying on people.'

'Alicia, you can't say that about a holy man of the cloth.'

'How does Mary McIlroy know?'

'She's his housekeeper and he confides in her.'

'I bet they get up to all sorts of...'

'Alicia...don't say something that will put another black mark on your soul. God forbid. You're in enough trouble.'

'Father Rooney said he wouldn't tell if we confessed and done our penance. He's a liar.'

'And did you?'

'Did I what?' Alicia asked.

'Did you confess and do your penance?'

'I still have to finish my penance. I've three more rosaries to say.' Alicia answered.

'When your exams are over you can take time out of school and help me in the shop. The business belongs to you after all.'

'I want to go to college. I've already applied for...'

'Let me back into the driving seat. We need to go before security arrives. They'll be none too pleased, and what with the skid marks you've left on the concrete.'

'Mammy you can't...'

'No Alicia...I won't hear any more on the matter. There are some things in this world that people learn to accept. God knows I had to accept that I was left on my own to rear a child. But there are some things that can never be accepted, because, they're wrong. You can't be kissing a girl, for the love of God. Who ever heard of such carry on?'

Alicia began to cry. They got out of the car. Alicia continued to sniffle while Sarah rummaged through the contents of her handbag for a tissue.

'Wipe your eyes and your nose on that, love.' Sarah said and gave Alicia the tissue.

They got back into the car again and Sarah was relieved to resume her role as driver.

'Click on your seat belt. Maybe we could open the shop late two evenings a week.' Sarah said as she started the car. 'That was your idea, remember?'

'When will the airport be finished?' Alicia asked.

'God only knows, they can't even decide on the name. Knock Airport or Monsignor Horan Airport or...'

'How about Monsignor Junior!' Alicia interjected.

'For the love of God, I'll have no more talk against the clergy. Do you want me six feet under in a box!' Sarah was breathless.

'I'm sorry mammy, but they've double standards.'

'That's their business. It's nothing to do with the likes

of us. Look, love, a lot of shops open late nowadays, and we should move with the times.' Sarah said. 'We'll finish your three rosaries tonight. You'll feel much better tomorrow. Your penance will be done. We all make silly mistakes. The best thing to do is put all this behind you.'

Alicia bowed her head as if in prayer and her heart felt heavy. Sarah manoeuvred the car out of the airport and onto the county road. She dreaded meeting any security employees arriving for the nightshift. She sped up a little and her handbag fell off the roof of the car and into a ditch.

Legal Harassment

Loretta Callaghan gazed across the antique mahogany desk at her new client. Declan McGinley was chewing gum. Disgruntled male. 40. Recently separated. WLTM solicitor for occasional court excursion and letter writing campaign to harass ex-partner. Declan made an incessant clicking sound with his tongue. If it was Friday afternoon it might not be so noticeable but Monday morning exacerbated the minutiae. Loretta was irritated, but she could easily fake enough empathy to put the client at ease.

'Your ex-partner's behaviour is unreasonable.' Loretta nodded her head self-assuredly. This motion sent approval signals to encourage the punter. She sniffed confidently. 'I've dealt with similar cases, Mr McGinley. A Court Order will resolve the matter. You absolutely need a formal access arrangement.' Loretta picked up a fountain pen, an action designed to portray her as pro-active. It wouldn't take much to reel him in.

'Call me Declan,' Declan said extending his arm across the desk, he shook Loretta's hand. 'There's no talking to Teresa.' Declan raised both hands in the air. The gesture reminded Loretta of an Egyptian hieroglyph. She absentmindedly doodled the matchstick symbol onto a document on her desk then quickly scored it out.

'That woman's impossible. She would drive you to drink.' Declan continued.

Loretta thought about contacting Emma, to meet up for a glass of wine after work.

Bodega was patronized by members of the legal profession, accountants, city council staff and other suit wearing professionals. Impromptu meetings, counsel, *jurisprudence-off-duty* and gossip was exchanged over a cocktail or a glass of house red. The food was from the organic low-fat menu. However, the low-fat option didn't keep the calorie intake at a minimum. The wine contained seven calories a gram, while a five-ounce glass of wine contained the same number of calories as a piece of chocolate. Loretta sighed, rubbed her stomach and picked up her mobile phone with her left hand. She typed a quick text to Emma. When she looked up after hitting the send option, Declan was still talking.

'You know what I mean...Teresa dictates all arrangements. She expects me to believe the children make their own decisions. All the decisions are made to suit her and her boyfriend. I'm not stupid.'

'When people separate, new partners bring extra complications.' Loretta could have had the conversation with the wall.

'How do we proceed? I mean, how can we move this

situation forward?' Declan removed the chewing gum from his mouth and held it up as if it was an exhibit. 'Bin?' He asked.

Loretta reached beneath the desk, lifted a wastepaper basket and held it out at arm's length. Declan felt the tension ease in his body as he discarded the gum, and sunk back into the conference room chair.

'Simple. We petition the court. We apply for a hearing date...a summons will be issued to your...ex-wife.'

'Will it be delivered by a member of the police force?' Declan asked trying not to sound excited.

'Let's focus on the necessary details.' Loretta said. 'The children stay with you one night per week.'

'Yes.'

'Friday or Saturday?'

'Friday.'

'And you want this to be reduced?'

'Yes.'

'To one night every two weeks?'

'That's right. I'm not an unpaid babysitting service.'

Loretta rubbed her forehead while scribbling a few notes on an A4 sheet of paper. Maybe she would buy a cherry tree for her front garden. They are so beautiful when they are in blossom. But then again, the blossoms never lasted long. Also, it would be an all too obvious reminder of the street where she and her associates had offices. Chancery Parade, *where everybody knows your claim,* was lined with cherry trees. In a city, the location and view was akin to a sea front property. Loretta snorted through her nose, a pair of shoes might be a more prudent purchase. A comfortable peep-toe with a kitten heel would be appropriate for a Monday morning come-down. Loretta momentarily removed her foot from her shoe and stretched her toes. She was cognizant of the tension on the ball of her foot. She wanted to reach down and rub the sole but instead she raised her eyes to check the strategically placed clock, behind her client's head. She needed to prolong the interview to tally up an adequate consultation fee.

The telephone on the desk rang. Loretta glimpsed through the reinforced glass panel where Phillipa her secretary gave a jumbled hand signal. Loretta picked up the receiver.

'Raul Campbell's on hold. The Children's Court Officer is running amok with the Logan children over interviews. He's insistent that you speak with him. He used the word 'now', Phillipa gave a short laugh. 'He's his usual aggressive self. What d'you think?' Phillipa was a powerhouse secretary.

'Blast him. Thanks, Phillipa. Go on put him through,' Loretta held her hand over the transmitter and mouthed the word 'sorry' to Declan.

'Hello Raul. You wanted to speak to me urgently?'

'You didn't return my call, Friday.' Raul's voice was irritable.

'Too busy, plus an emergency case took priority.'

'We have to push forward on the Logan case. It's in stalemate too long.'

'I realise that the children have missed three interviews...you don't seem to take on board that they are upset meeting you.'

Loretta stared directly at Declan as she listened to Raul Campbell. Declan pursed his lips and listened intently.

'I understand the children's father hasn't seen them for a month. I can't force any child to attend a court officer meeting...' Loretta tapped her fingers on the desk.

'You could help me on this one. Get Mrs Logan to comply. If I have my reports done, the case can move out of limbo. Judges work quicker with documentation in place.'

'I'm with a client,' Loretta shook her head. 'Raul, when you met the Logan children the impact was negative for them. I wish to go ahead without any Children's Court Officer reports. You met them once. Base your report on that. Mrs Logan is happy enough at present with full access. The ball's in your court. Gotta go. Bye.'

Loretta hung up the phone.

'Apologies Declan...you were saying that Una is...'

'Who's Una?' Declan asked bewildered.

'Your ex-wife...the mother of your three children.'

'Two children...and her name is Teresa.'

Loretta stood up and took a few steps across the office to the tall rectangular window. She stared dreamily at the cherry trees in full bloom brandishing delicate pink flowers. Declan continued talking but Loretta didn't register an iota of his monologue. She licked her tongue across her front teeth and felt the streak of lipstick.

'Oh, how very Saturday night,' she chuckled to herself and scraped her teeth with a finger nail. Loretta hoped the lipstick streak was the result of reapplying it hastily after elevenses. She cringed at the thought of it being there on her arrival at work, at the same time as her senior associates.

'...and now she says I'll have to make a contribution to the school uniforms...I gave her fifty quid last week towards some imaginary...'

'Are there other issues that I should be aware of?' Loretta twirled around clumsily. She wanted to examine her client's reaction and her snap question caused him to raise his left leg and rest the foot on his right knee, creating the figure-four.

'Issues? What do you mean?' Declan stammered as he hunched forward and grabbed his left leg with both hands.

'Domestic abuse? Mental abuse? Did you manage the finances when you were a couple? Did you tell her what to wear? Did you restrict her movements? Did you ever drive too fast to scare her?'

'Certainly not.' Declan interrupted. 'I'm the injured party here,' He was resolute.

'Look, relax, I have to ask. It's not personal.' Loretta exhaled loudly. In due course there would be accusations of unreasonable conduct. She would vehemently deny them on behalf of her client. He was unequivocally a devoted father.

'Are you a gambler Mr McGinley?'

'The occasional flutter on the Saturday fixtures.'

'What about alcohol? Drugs?'

'No more than the average person. Well, I mean alcohol...certainly no drugs. Well, nothing hardcore. What's your definition of drugs?'

'Don't worry...it should be straight forward.' Loretta added knowing that Declan would never be happy with any negotiations or outcome during the court hearings. He would be a regular feature in her office for the next few years.

Phillipa entered the office carrying a bundle of documents. She held a pen between her teeth.

'Sorry, Loretta I need your signature on this before I lodge it with the Court Clerk.' Phillipa's voice was muffled.

Some papers slipped out of a folder and hit Declan on the head. He picked them up and set them on the desk.

Loretta and Phillipa pored over the documents while they whispered, nodded, exchanged distorted facial expressions, tut-tutted and sighed. Phillipa gathered up the documents again.

'Oh, one other thing, Mr Deeney rang.' Phillipa's voice was apologetic. 'He cancelled his 3.15pm appointment.' She hesitated, then added. 'He and his ex-wife have come to an agreement over the sale of the property.'

'Call him back immediately.' Loretta waved her pen in the air. Tell him I want to reschedule a meeting. I strongly advise against any action until then.'

'Will do, straight away. And Jim Murphy has arrived.'

'We're finishing here. Hold on going to the courthouse. I need you to file an application for Declan here, before close of business.'

Loretta looked at Declan as he unwrapped another stick of gum and stuffed it into his mouth.

'Declan, I'll set the wheels in motion. We'll be in touch as soon as the hearing date has been confirmed.'

'Do you need me to do anything in the mean time?'

'Go home, relax and don't be concerned. You've absolutely nothing to worry about.'

Declan stood up, and they shook hands and he left the office.

Loretta moved to the window and continued to stare out at the busy street as her next client entered. She watched Declan cross the road without looking left or right. The cherry blossoms fell like confetti at his feet.

'Hello Loretta.' Jim Murphy said loudly. 'I can't believe the divorce has finally come through! You're an absolute star.'

'You've every reason to smile, Jim. You've been through the wars.'

'The battle of Trafalgar, Gettysburg and Stalingrad rolled into one.' Jim chuckled.

Loretta pressed her lips together in a satisfied grimace.

'I've the Decree Nisi for you. The Decree Absolute will follow in approximately six to eight weeks.'

'I don't know how to thank you, Loretta.' Jim stretched his hand across the desk.

'Just doing my job. But I told you that you would have to be patient.' Loretta presented Jim with the document. He smiled noting the red stamp of officialdom: High Court of Justice in Her Majesty's Court for Divorce and Matrimonial Causes.

Jim's lips parted and he attempted to laugh but fell short.

'I had my legal file out this morning. I could wallpaper the house from top to bottom with it!' Jim said.

'Your case was particularly acrimonious.'

'The children are old enough now to make their own decisions about access.' Jim said and his expression became serious. 'I didn't realise the first day I walked into this office that it would take six years before I'd see the back of all this! No offence intended.'

'None taken. I wish you all the best Jim. I'm gonna miss you,' Loretta cleared her throat and licked her tongue across her teeth. 'You've had to put your life on hold for quite a few years. Your new partner has been very tolerant.

'Ah, she's an understanding woman alright. Stood by me through thick and thin.' Jim chuckled.

'Well,' Loretta said. 'Now you both can finally fix a date for your wedding.'

***

Loretta was reassured as she gazed into the compact mirror taken from her handbag. There was no lipstick showing on her top teeth. The first day of the working week had been shockingly busy. She thought about her new client with his nervous expression, a flustered first-timer employing the legal process for access to his children. She had been recommended to him by word-of-mouth. Her reputation as a family law solicitor was in good shape. She decided against the cherry tree. What about a *Chinese Willow*? That might force her to have a garden pond put in at some stage. A few more office chores and she could break for *Bodega*. Hopefully Emma would have grabbed a table by the window.

The New Caravan

The snowfall turned the sky grey and soft flakes formed a white layer on top of the parked cars, on the rubbish bins and on the boundary wall that enclosed the hospice. The snow that hit the ground melted into watery slush.

Rita shivered but was relieved to feel the damp air on her face. The heat inside the building was stifling. She had been awake all night and had quietly slipped outside to the smoking area. Rita was fantasizing about the new caravan when the palliative care nurse called her name from the reception doorway. Rita inhaled deeply and stubbed out the cigarette in the sand filled ashtray. During her moment of absence from her friend's bedside, Anne had died. The shock was unbearable.

'I can't explain what it's like,' Rita said a week later to her daughter who dropped by to ask her for money.

'I only need thirty-five pounds until Thursday lunchtime.' Siobhan interrupted.

'When you have no-one to share with, what good is anything?' Rita said and opened her purse giving Siobhan two twenty-pound notes.

'The funeral's over Mammy. You'll have to let her go. I know it's hard, she was your best friend but...'

'The caravan was all we ever wanted. You know what your daddy was like. Anne's lump of a man was no better. We never expected anything from either of them. And when you lot where reared...'

'You don't need to explain that to me. Look Mammy, what choice do you have? You must keep going, Anne would want you to...'

'We thought we'd find peace in the caravan.' Rita said.

'The house is quiet, and you've extra money now that you're not buying the caravan.'

'I couldn't afford to buy it on my own. The house is lonely. The caravan was going to be different. But without Anne, what's the point?'

'Exactly.' Siobhan sighed. She removed her mobile phone from her handbag and flipped opened the diamante cover.

'Oh, 14:45. I can't be late picking the kids up. Look, I'll come back tomorrow and stay longer.'

Rita sunk into the high back armchair. The snow hadn't stopped falling since the night at the hospice and it now covered everything. Rita gazed toward the window and felt as if she was inside a snow-globe. She brushed her fingers through her dried-out perm. Her skin was coarse and had wrinkled prematurely. Anne had looked much younger and hadn't smoked a day in her life. Rita removed her thin rimmed glasses and held them in her fist. Anne had only known for a few days that she was terminally ill. She hadn't time to come to terms with the breast cancer diagnosis let alone think about dying.

Ductal carcinoma. Invasive. Higher Grade 3. It seems when you grow old you learn medical terms. Mammogram. Core biopsy. Surgery. Chemotherapy. Radiotherapy. Hormone therapy. Targeted therapy. There was no hopeful prognosis because Anne deteriorated quickly. No time for anything.

How can someone not be here anymore? Suddenly, and all at once, they're gone? How can a fifty-year-old woman be lying in a cemetery in the frozen ground? Rita lost her best friend, her only friend. You can't reach back into the past and grab hold of the important things.

Rita picked up the remote control and turned on the television. The noise blasted out and she switched it off. She went into the kitchen to make a cup of tea but couldn't remember what she'd gone in for. Rita went upstairs to the bedroom. She stood in the doorway and decided to lie down but instead she sat on the end of the bed, placed her face in her palms and slumped forward.

Rita wept.

Rita was exhausted and fell asleep on top of the bed. When she woke she felt a rush of energy. She didn't think about her dead friend or about the new caravan. She went downstairs and straight out the front door. The sky overhead was dense. The snowdrift here and there looked like a flutter of white butterflies, but Rita didn't notice. She hadn't put her coat on and she didn't notice that either. She walked aimlessly for a while. Then in the town centre she went into the bus station, bought a ticket and boarded a bus journeying to the coast. The journey was slow, the roads hazardous, but Rita was unconcerned and didn't feel the cold as she got off the bus and walked towards the caravan park. The owner was delighted to see her.

'Have you come alone today?' He asked. 'My solicitor said that the paperwork will be ready to sign in the next day or two.'

'I need to see it again, please?' Rita asked.

'You're not thinking about backing out on the deal? Like I said, this is the best maintained caravan park in this part of country. We're on a beautiful peninsula, and the views come second to the people. We look out for each other. You'll be in good company.'

Rita stared beyond him out towards the bitter sea. If it wasn't for the mountains it would be difficult to know where the water ended and the sky began.

'I want one more look,' she said.

The park owner nodded and Rita followed him down a gravel pathway that cut through rows of well-kept holiday and residential caravans. Some of the caravans had elaborate decking and colourful plant pots with bulbs pushing green shoots upwards out of their snowy bedspreads. The owner fidgeted with a fat bunch of keys and when they stopped, he opened the door to the caravan with the correct key.

Rita went inside the caravan by herself. She looked at the little wooden galley kitchen and the small dinette area. Anne didn't like the brown stretch covers on the foam seating at the front. They had definite plans to reupholster. Rita recalled talking about it the day they decided that this would be their caravan and the terrible sadness returned.

'What good is the caravan if I'm alone?' Rita said. 'I may as well be in a hole in the ground.'

***

'When you get to my age, life no longer gives you anything.' Rita told Siobhan the following day. 'I had a beautiful friend. A soulmate. Now I have nothing.'

'Mammy. You can't let grief take over your life. There are other things to live for.'

'How can you move on when all you have is despair?'

'You're depressed. Your best friend died.' Siobhan said and tried to sound compassionate. 'You need a bit of time, that's all. Oh, I won't be able to give you that money back until the start of the week.'

Siobhan left and when she closed the front gate, she turned around and looked at the house. Her mother had pushed the net curtain aside and was staring out the window. Siobhan smiled and raised her hand to wave but Rita didn't notice.

***

On Monday morning, Siobhan stood in the Post Office queue. She was glad to be inside. The snow had started to thaw, the ground was wet, the trees dripped and the sun was a giant bead of amber.

Siobhan's phone rang and she fumbled inside her handbag to retrieve it. The incoming number was her mother's, but when she answered the voice of a man spoke.

'Hello, am...sorry...can you hear me...yes,' the man

coughed harshly. 'I'm out walking here and found this phone on the New Bridge. There's personal belonging too, a handbag and some photographs. Can you hear me? Yes.' The man's voice was strained. 'Your number was the last number dialled. By any chance do you know the person that owns this phone?'

Brief Encounter

Mona had to be drunk before she could have sex with her husband Steve. Every Friday and Saturday night she would get pissed on cheap white wine and hope that Steve would get it 'over and done with' as quickly as possible. They were married twenty-two years. Mona couldn't figure out why or when her feelings of sexual repulsion began, but she drank the wine to anesthetise them.

'Was it after the first baby?' Mona asked herself as she mopped the toilet floor in the shopping centre. It was a busy Saturday evening and a late-night shift for her. 'I'm so bloody tired.' Mona said to herself and shuddered at the thought of Steve's eager hands hoping to encourage her to reciprocate. 'I'm always bloody tired.'

Saturday was the busiest day in the shopping centre and the cleaning company that employed her were liable to do impromptu 'spot checks'. Mona kept her head down.

She dragged the mop from one side to the other, over the tiled floor in the ladies' room. She thought the mop resembled a giant squid that could attack and devour the never-ending queue that didn't ease back until closing.

Why do people waiting in a queue look so sad? Mona thought. Maybe it's disgust. Sometimes it's hard to tell the difference between sadness and disgust.

'That toilet needs loo paper.' An elderly woman proclaimed loudly. She was dragging a wheelie shopping trolley bag which bumped against the door of the cubicle. 'It's that last cubicle, love.' She said to Mona. 'Luckily I had tissues in my handbag.'

Mona pushed the maintenance trolley forward. She removed the loo roll from the under cart and went into the cubicle to refill the locked paper dispenser. Once the task was completed, Mona shuffled the trolley backwards and nodded towards the toilet cubicle to let those waiting know that it was available for use again. She didn't want eye contact with anyone. Mona was trying to decide which she hated most, cleaning toilets or having sex with Steve.

It shouldn't be like this, Mona thought to herself. How can a relationship that began with desire and sexual attraction just fade...how can something that once meant the whole world not matter anymore? There must be something broken inside me. This can't be Steve's fault. He's still attracted to me.

Three teenage girls came into the toilets and were singing loudly. Mona didn't look up. They too were a regular feature on any given Saturday afternoon.

'Hey Louise, you should write something about you and Paul on the toilet wall!' A lofty girl called to her friend and threw her an indelible maker.

Louise caught it, and at the same time she caught sight of her mother.

'Why don't you draw a picture of what he showed you last night!' The girls giggled and looked boldly at the people in the queue. They had no difficulty with eye contact.

'I don't want to write anything.' Louise said.

'Here give it to me then...we should do a score chart.'

The lofty girl grabbed the marker off Louise and was about to draw a line on the wall when Mona stepped forward.

'You can't write on the wall.'

'How many times did you score last week, Louise?' The lofty girl ignored Mona.

'I'll have to ask you to leave.' Mona said.

'Who are you? The bouncer!' The lofty girl said in a mocking tone and her other friend laughed encouragingly. Louise didn't laugh.

'No, I'm not the bouncer...but if you write on that wall, I'll have to clean it, and I have enough work to do.'

'But that's your job! You clean other people's shit!' The lofty girl was nasal and mocking.

'Hey,' Louise said to her friend. 'Let's get out of here. These toilets are full of germs. I want to go somewhere else.'

The lofty girl stared at Mona as she defiantly removed the marker cap and placed the chisel tip against the wall. She continued to stare as she dragged the indelible marker along the wall and towards the exit. The girls left the toilets.

Mona got the anti-graffiti wipes from her maintenance trolley and removed the dark line. She would say nothing to Louise about the incident when she got home. It was just bravado. The girls wanted to feel grown up.

Mona removed the cleaning rota record sheet from its display frame, she signed her initials and noted the time. She would check the toilets on the ground floor and be back again in half an hour. A few more hours and the working day would be done.

Mona rattled the maintenance trolley forward and out of the toilets. It just about fitted through the door fame. As she pushed it towards the staff elevator she remembered that the M&S off-licence on the ground floor of the shopping centre were advertising *three for two* offers on selected white wines.

Best Writers Come from Massachusetts

'The best writers come from Massachusetts.' Michael spoke loudly, certain that nobody at any of the other tables in the restaurant could convince him otherwise. 'Creative energy, an electromagnetic resonance that comes straight from the heartbeat of the earth!'

Caroline faked a laugh. It came out as a snort and ended in a grunt. She had heard Michael say this on numerous occasions. It was usually delivered after his first sip from his third glass of red wine. It didn't matter about the company, the occasion or the location. Tonight, it was just her and Michael and he wasn't competing for air-time. The affirmation had come quicker than she expected. She wasn't sure how much of the speech she could tolerate. Caroline brushed a strand of light brown hair behind her ear, placed both elbows on the table and leaned forward.

'Can't we talk about something else, just for tonight?'

Michael looked confused. He too leant forward, mirroring Caroline's body language, they resembled opponents in a chess game.

'There's a tie in your soup.' Caroline said.

Michael's Burberry necktie licked the top of his bowl of carrot, onion and coriander soup. Caroline watched in disgust as it sank further and further into the gloop.

'What?' Michael looked down and fumbling picked up a napkin and used it to catch the excess liquid that dripped from the rescued necktie.

'Do you prefer company when we're dining out?' Caroline asked.

'Darling, it's good for us to have time on our own.'

'That's why we should talk about something different.'

They were suddenly silent. Caroline looked around the restaurant. Their "table for two" was near the bar while larger trendy parties were given window seats. The room was lit by candles in the centre square tables and a few blurry overhead lights that hung down by a fine thread. Floor to ceiling windows gave an unobtrusive view of the Bay and lights flickered in the background of the harbour.

'I feel like I have Ménière's Disease.' She said.

'Darling, don't be silly, you're perfectly fine.'

'If an artist must have a condition, why can't I, as a clean-living citizen, have some kind of malady or madness.'

'I didn't think you were interested in artists.'

'Well, I've no choice but to listen to your incessant conversations with Walter, the Poundian magician pulling cantos out of a hat. Ryan, the moody Golden Bough Yeatsian. Suzie your specialist in Medieval English Literature. Paul Manolis, lover of all things Greek, except feta cheese...and of course you and your Massaachusettsan loyalty.

'You could offer a seminar on *how to write one-line biographies*.' Michael was terse.

Caroline ignored him. She rested her chin on her hand and continued to look out the window.

'Darling, you gotta admit, it's a disproportionate number.' Michael began.

'What is?' Caroline asked. Her eyelashes fluttered rapidly.

'Well, the number of top-class writers that come from Massachusetts. You have of course Emerson, Dickinson, Hawthorne, Thoreau, the two Lowells, of course,' he paused. 'Cummings, Frost, Kerouac, and not forgetting Boston's bad boy Poe, for Christ's sake. We are talking about some of the most prominent...'

'I know! You've told me. Even Dr Bloody Suess! And you and that dreadful poem of yours where you recite all their names. It's like a rhyme for rope-skipping. All the years of studying writers...you haven't learned a damn thing!' Caroline said in exasperation.

'Darling, you can't deny that it has to be related to the landscape. It's no coincidence. It directed my thesis argument.'

'Look Michael, if I admit that you are one-hundred-per-cent correct, can we change the subject?'

'So, you don't agree?'

'You lecture about what you've never experienced. What do you know about landscape? When is the last time you even dipped your toe in a river!'

'The evidence...'

'We've had this conversation. I can't take it anymore!'

Caroline put her hands up to cover her ears.

The waiter came over to the table and the patrons slouched back gracelessly in their seats. The waiter began to clear dishes and cutlery from the first-course.

'Did Sir not like his soup? The waiter spoke with a strong North of Ireland accent.

Michael waved his hands insolently in the air.

'It was fine. Do what you need to do and bring the next course, please.'

'That was extremely rude.' Caroline snapped when the waiter was out of earshot. 'You're one of the rudest people I've ever met. I don't know why I hang around with academics. You have no concept of how difficult life can be for people who actually work for a living.' Caroline was once again animated and prodded the table with her index finger.

'Darling,' Michael rubbed his forehead, 'I'd just like to see it acknowledged. It's important to me.'

'You're still talking about writers from Massachusetts?' Caroline raised her voice. 'Will you pay the bill? I want to go. I'm going to visit mother for a couple of days. I'd like to have conversations about the weather, invasive rhododendrons, the best soap flakes and clothes driers, and, at what time her mail is delivered in the mornings. She has a special notebook, keeping tabs on the postman's schedule.'

'Your mother is crazy.'

'Everybody's mother is crazy!' Caroline bellowed.

'I think you're a little hysterical.'

'A little hysterical! You think hysteria comes in a range of sizes!'

The Irish waiter arrived with the lobster salads.

'The cockroach of the ocean.'

'Sir?' The waiter said.

'That's a Ryan comment.' Caroline said.

'Well, he's not here tonight to say it!' Michael replied. The waiter left hastily.

'And let's not forget Suzie, what would she say?'

'I know!' Michael emulated a high pitch screech, 'Suzie would say "*I can't eat a bottom feeder.*"'

'Which isn't reflected in her taste in men!' Caroline laughed, drawing Michael into the laughter.

'She sounds like that character from *Singing in the Rain.*' Michael snapped his fingers. 'What do you call her?'

'Lina Lamont.'

'Darling you have an excellent memory. I can't imagine any student sitting through one of Suzie's lectures. Can you conceive the works of Chaucer in that accent!'

'*And I cayn't stand'im.*' Caroline said and they laughed again.

'Darling,' Michael leaned forward and his voice was sincere. 'Please, don't go to your mother's. We have a fun-time together. Tell me, what would you like to talk about?'

'I'd like to make a decision about where we'll go on vacation. I want it to be just us. Please don't invite anyone else. No talk about suicidal poets, or what works were written in a lunatic asylum, or how many drafts does it take to complete a short story, or how Dylan Thomas was treated by the professors at Harvard or how Emerson was ousted! We haven't been away together, on our own, for such a long time.'

'Ok, just me and you Caroline,' Michael said and stabbed the salad leaves with his fork. 'Where would you like to go?'

Michael didn't expect to make any further contribution to the conversation. The salad needed considerable chewing. He would take the opportunity to ruminate. Caroline pretended she was making the plans up as she went along. He had been caught; hook, line and sinker. She'd probably already consulted a travel advisor.

'I had an idea that we could go to the Grand Canyon.'

Michael choked on a piece of lobster meat. He tried to sit upright, and in a panic slapped his chest repeatedly with his fist. He stood up and his chair fell sideways onto the floor. Michael put both hands to his throat as his face turned blue.

'Oh my God,' Caroline called out terrified. 'First aider. Is there a first aider in the restaurant?'

The Irish waiter appeared from the kitchen with a plate of mussels which he quickly set on the bar. He stood behind Michael and placed his left hand beneath his diaphragm and with his right hand gave him five strong blows on his back. The obstruction didn't clear. Michael continued to struggle for breath. The waiter put both hands around him, and made a sharp abdominal thrust. The piece of lobster meat dislodged and fell onto the plate, it looked like the dissected remains of a tonsillectomy. Michael dropped to the ground, and was kneeling before the waiter.

Caroline knelt beside him.

'Darling, thank goodness you're okay.'

'Listen folks, hey everyone, return to your tables. He's fine. He just needs some fresh air.' The waiter smiled at the customers. 'Sir, come to the balcony. Follow me. I'll get you a glass of water, and we can make sure that you don't need any medical attention.'

The air was chilly outside and Michael shook involuntarily.

'It's shock, darling.' Caroline said and put her arm around him.

The wooden decking was damp and they sat at a metal table. Yellow and orange lights from nearby buildings seemed to drip into the harbour like melting candle wax. The waiter brought a glass of water and gave them their coats.

'How do you feel, Sir? The manager wants to know. He can phone for a doctor, if you wish?'

'We're fine, thank you' Caroline said looking completely relaxed. 'It was a Freudian choke!'

The waiter left and Michael stared at Caroline blankly.

'Why the Grand Canyon?' He asked knowing there was no persuasive argument that could possibly convince him to go.

'I thought we could take a road-trip. It's the kind of thing you often talk about…the kind of thing that writers do. I even thought we could hire a Winnebago.'

'It would use up all our vacation time. I couldn't commit to the driving.'

'But you went there when you were a student. I never got to go.' Caroline sounded like a child.

'We could fly. Darling, I want you to be happy. I want us, to be happy. You're having some sort of mid-life breakdown, aren't you?'

'I want to see the Grand Canyon and you think I'm having a breakdown!'

'I never heard you mention the Canyon before. It's out of the blue and comes as a shock, that's all.' Michael rubbed his throat.

'What about Russian writers?' Caroline said defiantly.

'Russian writers. What do you mean?'

'Russian writers are awesome. China has great canons of literature. Japan, Spain, France. Wow, those guys could really write. But what would I know? I'm a high school teacher and not fit for Mount PhD Rushmore.'

'I'm referencing writers whose first language is English.'

'You never mentioned that as a stipulation,' Caroline began to cry.

'Darling, what's the matter?' Michael asked.

'It's the first night in a long time that we have dined out alone and I thought it would be different.'

'Different from what?'

'Different from the usual conversations.'

'Conversation is never predetermined, one topic leads to another.'

'Do you know what they say about us when we're not around? For all we know they lied about having "family commitments" tonight. I have been thinking about it, and maybe we shouldn't be so dependent on other people's company.'

'Caroline, you're being crazy again. We know these people most of our life.'

The waiter returned and looking at Caroline he noticed that she had been crying.

'Sir? Is sir is feeling much better, I hope? Is there anything else I can do for you folks? Can I bring the desserts menu?'

'Desserts is stressed.'

'Pardon?' The waiter said. 'I don't understand.'

'The word desserts if spelt backwards becomes

stressed!' Caroline explained.

'Oh, I see,' the waiter said. 'I never knew that. So, I can bring you the desserts menu?'

'You're Irish.' Michael said.

'I am, sir.'

'How long have you been in Boston?'

'Four months, sir.'

'Have you seen us in here before?'

'I have, sir. Mostly on a Friday night.'

'Are we always in company?'

'You are, sir. I don't understand the question, sir.'

'Well, do we look happy?'

'Tonight, sir?'

'No. When we are in company.'

'Very happy, sir.'

'And, what about tonight?'

'Well, you look a bit stressed tonight.'

'So, in company, we look happy?'

'Yes, sir. Shall I bring the desserts menu?'

'No thanks,' Caroline said. 'Can we just have the bill please.'

The waiter left.

'We work such long hours, and our down-time is spent sleeping or in restaurants with the faculty. I feel like an accessory. They wouldn't want to know me if it wasn't for you.'

'They really like you.'

'They do?'

'Of course, they do. They always beg me to invite you. They tell me I'm dull on my own.'

'But we shouldn't be dull when we're on our own!'

'Darling, we've had such a lovely evening. I won't

mention writers from Massachusetts again,' Michael touched her cheek.

'But it's your thing. You always need to talk about it.'

'There are other great writers and great literatures out there...it's not good to be so limited.'

'No darling, I disagree. You must stick with what you love.'

The waiter re-appeared and placed the bill on the table.

'Hey, would you recommend a holiday in Ireland?' Michael asked the waiter.

'I would indeed, sir. Really beautiful. The coastline is stunning. And, of course, the best writers in the world come from Ireland.

'The best writers come from Massachusetts.' Caroline snapped at the waiter.

Michael quickly wrote the cheque. He fumbled in his pocket, took out a handful of dollars and gave the waiter a generous tip.

***

In the taxi, the driver said nothing and they said nothing. Caroline thought about returning to the apartment that was laden and strewn with books. She stared out the window at the neon signs. The streets became faculty corridors. She saw the city as a vast campus in the middle of a never ending semester. And, Massachusetts had become ten times bigger. She looked at him in the taxi beside her. He had opened a shirt button so that he could polish his glasses as if sharpening his sword ready for battle.

NOTE ON THE AUTHOR

Pamela Mary Brown *Writer-in-Residence* HMP Magilligan. Creative Writing Tutor-Assessor, North West Regional College. Poet-founder of Poetry Chicks performed extensively in Ireland/UK; Workshops and Creative Writing Facilitator at public venues, schools and institutions in Ireland/UK; studied Community Drama, University of Ulster; Media Studies at the Foyle Arts Centre, Derry. BA (Hons) Degree in English Literature and Creative Writing.

An Irish Lullaby (2015) novel. *The Fag* Short Film Award (Clones) 2009 (co-writer). *A Rainy Climate* (1994) play Edinburgh Festival. *'Til Death do us Part* (1993) play *The Playhouse*, Derry.

Short fiction/poetry publishing credits *AvantAppalachia* ezine (2016/17) *Fiction Feast* (UK, 2015); *The SHop* (co-translations of Ezra Pound into Irish, 2012); *Decanto* (UK, 2011); *Spleen* (Manchester, 2011); *Beautiful Scruffiness* (UK, 2009); *Citizen32* (Manchester,2009); *AlphabeTitudes* (Guildhall Press, 2007); *Speech Therapy* (Belfast, 2007); *EVE* (Guildhall Press, 2006); *The Eye of the Horse*: Poetry and Photography Exhibition 22 Poems, with photographs by Jan Voster 1999; *Tight* (USA, 1998); *Lucid Moon* (USA May & August 1997); *The Foam Sprite* (1995).

89444916R00080

Made in the USA
Columbia, SC
21 February 2018